"There must be something I can do."

Miranda watched with growing vexation as Peter paced the floor and considered her future with all the passion of a cleric. Suddenly, he stopped and rounded on her.

"Dash it all, Miranda!" he declared. "I will marry you myself!"

As Peter strode purposefully towards her, Miranda's voice made him stop.

"No," she said with just a tell-tale quiver. "I will not marry you. I do not know why you ever supposed that I would."

Peter froze. "Not marry me? I do not understand."

"You do not?" Miranda's face had gone red, and her eyes were strangely bright. "I suppose I should be very grateful for the offer, but I am not! In fact, I would not marry you if you were the last man in England!" So saying, she gave a great sob and rushed from the room, leaving Peter to wonder if the end of the world had come.

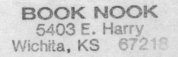

THE MARRIAGE BROKERS

IRENE NORTHAN

Harlequin Books

TORONTO • NEW YORK • LONDON
AMSTERDAM • PARIS • SYDNEY • HAMBURG
STOCKHOLM • ATHENS • TOKYO • MILAN

Reprinted with the permission of Robert Hale Limited
First published in Great Britain 1983

Harlequin Regency Romance edition published January 1991
ISBN 0-373-31142-7

THE MARRIAGE BROKERS

Printed in U.S.A.

CHAPTER ONE

"SIR, YOU CANNOT be serious!" Richard Branscombe stared at his parent, his handsome face puckered in horror. "I implore you, say that you are joking, or feeling a trifle bosky, or that your mind is to let—anything, only do not say that you are serious."

Sir Henry faced him squarely and with unusual resolution.

"But I am serious," he said firmly. "If you wish me to pay your debts then you must find a husband for Miranda. That is my condition. And do unscrew your face, twisting it so will produce wrinkles more swiftly than anything else."

"But it is so unreasonable!" Richard protested, obediently relaxing his facial skin. "I will do anything within my power, aye and gladly, but to find a husband for Miranda ... Dash it all, Papa, that is too much. I think the world of her, you know that. No fellow ever had a better sister. But a husband! That is asking the impossible."

"Impossible or not, those are my terms." It was rare for Sir Henry to be so determined, but he was a worried man and fast becoming a desperate one. Something of his anxiety transmitted itself to his son.

"Why are you in such a pother all of a sudden, sir? After all, she has sailed through four Seasons without getting near matrimony and you have never seemed troubled out of the ordinary. Why all the pandemonium now?"

"It was five Seasons," Sir Henry corrected him absently. "And the reason for the pandemonium, as you call it, is because I am certain I have detected a growing similarity between Miranda and your Great-Aunt Evangeline."

"No!" As a child Richard had been chastened by tales of his Great-Aunt Evangeline as other children were by threats of gypsies or Bonaparte.

"Yes! She was before your time, my boy, yet even after five-and-twenty years memories of your Great-Aunt still cause me to shudder. She had not the slightest idea of what was right or proper. You cannot imagine the distress she caused the family with her ways, tramping about the countryside, her pockets filled with bread and cheese, talking to the most unsuitable people, and handing out religious tracts to anyone she met. Your grandfather always maintained it was an unfortunate consequence of her Christian name, and he could have been right. She had a tame magpie, you know, which used to sit on her shoulder, and its behaviour was, to put it delicately, unsociable in the extreme, not to say insanitary, yet Evangeline did not care. But worst of all her faults she had a dreadful fancy for yellow stockings. Bright yellow worsted stockings!'' Sir Henry closed his eyes at the recollection.

"How dreadful!" Richard recoiled before such an appalling lack of taste. "And you are convinced that Miranda is following in her footsteps? Might you not be imagining things because of your anxiety to see her wed?"

"I am not mistaken, my boy. For one thing, she has a fledgling jackdaw in her sitting room. Says it fell from its nest and that she is rearing it, but jackdaw or magpie, you can see where such things lead."

"Yes, back to Great-Aunt Evangeline. I now begin to understand the urgency of the situation."

"I am glad you do, for if Miranda continues in her gothic ways it will mean social ruin for the pair of us, dear boy, nothing less. Kinship with Evangeline proved a great strain on us all, I recall.

"And you see marriage as the only remedy?"

"Unless you can think of some alternative. It has been my experience that Society at large regards anyone connected with an eccentric spinster with great suspicion, whereas, if the lady is married, no matter how odd her behaviour, folk merely feel rather sorry for her husband."

"I see what you mean," said Richard, who was struck with admiration at this unexpected bout of reasoning from his father.

"I am glad you do, my boy." Sir Henry beamed with pride at his only son, so like himself twenty years ago, the same lithe figure, the same handsome face, the same innate elegance. The handsomest man in the country they had called Henry Branscombe then, a title he had happily relinquished in turn to his son. Not that the years had been unkind to him, there had been no thickening of his waist, no drooping of his jowls, just a little silvering of his dark hair which looked *très distingué*. Only a slight lack of inches marred the manly perfection of both father and son. It puzzled Sir Henry that the deity to whom he had fervently prayed to supply those missing inches had mischievously given them all to Miranda. The marks on the schoolroom door where he had so fondly measured the height of his children had been abandoned when Miranda's neared six feet.

"I am glad that you understand," repeated Sir Henry, "for that brings us back to your debts. Two thousand pounds would seem to be rather a large sum to require in a hurry."

"It is only one debt, Papa, and it is a matter of honour."

"Honour eh? You lost it all in some wager?"

"Not exactly. I got in a bit deep playing cards, and Peter bailed me out."

"Young Kerswell? And he is dunning you? I thought he was a particular friend of yours."

"He is, and of course he is not dunning me!" Richard looked aghast at the idea. "In fact he has never mentioned the money at all, but I happen to know that his pockets are to let at the moment and he has the chance of a marvellous business venture, so he needs all the blunt he can raise."

"If I know young Kerswell the business venture will have four legs attached, which means that his father will not help him."

"Well, you know Sir John's views on horse racing."

"I do indeed, and I have a certain sympathy with them. How young Kerswell can be so fond of the Turf is more than I can fathom. The people are usually so outlandish in their dress, and their neckwear is invariably frightful. However, this does put a different complexion on things. Peter Kerswell did help you out of a predicament, did he not?" Up till now Sir Henry had been quite proud of his own resolve, but now he felt it begin to disintegrate about him. "I mean, it is scarcely fair that the fellow should lose by it."

"No, it is not fair," agreed Richard hopefully.

"Perhaps I ought to pay your debt at once after all. But if I do then you must still consider yourself honour bound by my condition."

"You mean that I have still to find a husband for Miranda?"

"Certainly I do."

"Oh Papa!" Richard's reply was more of a wail. "But that is an impossible task. She is—I mean she—she lacks beauty."

"Put it bluntly, boy. Miranda is plain."

"She is more than plain, Papa, she is the plainest girl I have ever set eyes on. I am most grateful to you for settling my debt, but you drive a cruel bargain. Still, I suppose I must do my best.''

After Richard had left the room Sir Henry wondered if he had indeed been a little too hard on the boy. As his thoughts wandered to his daughter with her ungainly figure, her lack of grace and her bewildering yet total absence of elegance, he was forced to suppress a groan. Finding a husband for such a creature would be hard indeed. Had he not tried desperately for these five long years? Yet it had to be done while she still had youth at least on her side. Her birthday was fast approaching, she would be four-and-twenty, a most significant age. To have her turn into a second Great-Aunt Evangeline was a Rubicon beyond which no prospective husband could be expected to pass.

''Though she is plain Miranda will make some man an excellent wife,'' said Sir Henry aloud. ''She is kind and affectionate as well as being practised in all matters of household management. Besides which she is intelligent, well informed and—and—'' Here Sir Henry faltered in his attempt to describe his daughter's more eccentric attributes in their best light. ''. . . and original!'' he finished triumphantly.

Meanwhile Richard had set off across the park of Branscombe Hall, his father's note for two thousand pounds in his pocket and a bemused expression on his handsome face. He was relieved that his father had settled the debt so promptly, for inconveniencing his friend, Peter, had distressed him greatly, but now he was equally distressed by the stringent condition Sir Henry had put upon the transaction. Richard's intellect, never particularly strong, succumbed entirely to this new strain put upon it. He felt there was only one thing he could do. It was what he always did in a crisis—consult his best friend, Peter Kerswell.

The Kerswells were the immediate neighbours of the Branscombes, members of the *nouveau riche*, for Sir John was a banker of great ability. He was able a man of more than passing discretion, for he had politely declined all offers of a peerage pressed upon him by grateful and impecunious members of Higher Orders, settling instead for a modest baronetcy. This rank was high enough to offer an *entrée* into Society for his large family without upsetting the sensibilities of the *haut ton*. Many years earlier he had moved to New Park, the estate adjoining Branscombe Hall, and proceeded to enjoy a life-style so full of taste and elegance that Sir Henry Branscombe had not the slightest hesitation in permitting his children to associate with his new neighbour's offspring. Of the numerous Kerswell progeny it was the only son, Peter, who was the particular friend of both Richard and Miranda.

So it was that Richard Branscombe now walked through the rolling Devon parkland on a path so well known to him from childhood—the short cut between the two estates. He walked with neat light steps, the soft leather of his gleaming high boots immaculate—from an early age he had had the ability to emerge unscathed from the rural hazards of thick mud and bovine residue. For once, he had no need to go up to the house in search of his friend, for he found him in the garden gazing intently at the top of the terrace wall. At his approach Peter looked up and beamed.

"'Morning, Richard. You are looking very tip-top!" he greeting him. "But, then, when do you not? I am glad you came by just now. Would you care to embark upon a small wager? The New Park Thunderer against the Branscombe Beauty?"

"Wager? What is this? You have been buying some new horse-flesh?"

"Not this time. I fancied something on a smaller scale, caterpillar racing. It is the coming thing, I promise you." He pointed to the stone wall where two undistinguished-looking caterpillars were sunning themselves.

"Oh, you are funning!" Richard sometimes experienced difficulty in following his friend's whimsies. "No, I have not come on any frivolous errand, this matter is serious."

"The devil it is!" Peter straightened up. He was a deal taller than his companion and could have presented almost as elegant an appearance if only he bothered, for he was broad-shouldered and long-limbed enough to have worn the latest fashions with distinction. Instead, he usually preferred the comfort of an old cloth frock-coat and a belcher kerchief tied casually about his neck.

"Now what is amiss, eh?" he asked.

By way of answer Richard handed him Sir Henry's bank-draft. Peter looked at it and colour rose in his face.

"Now there was no call for this!" he exclaimed. "I could have waited, you know."

"No you could not! You pruned your purse pretty thin helping me out the way you did, and I will not have you lose the chance of a share in that racing stable simply because you were good enough to pull me out of the mire. Therefore I am repaying you with many thanks."

"I must admit it is a bit of business after my own heart. It is not every day a fellow gets the chance to buy a share in the nicest little string of fliers from here to Newmarket, but above all else I would not make things too hot for you with your father. Sir Henry did not cut up too rough, I hope."

"Well, yes and no."

"Now there is an answer remarkable for its clarity!"

"What I mean is, he did not bawl me out much, but he did set his condition upon the repayment."

"I hope he commanded you to forswear the card-table for the next thirty years. Believe me it would be for your own good. You are not set out to be a gamester, take my word for it. How you got involved with that last pack of wolves is more than I will ever know. Could you not see that they were a load of wrong 'uns? There were more signals flying about that card-game than the Navy telegraphs in a year. It was obvious that they were out to pluck the plumpest pigeon they could find.''

''Papa has not commanded me to forswear anything,'' retorted Richard, a little huffed to hear himself described as a pigeon. ''No, his condition concerns Miranda.''

''Miranda?''

''Yes. I am now honour bound to find a husband for her as soon as possible. Peter you must help me! I do not even know where to begin!''

'''Struth, I am not surprised,'' breathed Peter, then added hastily, ''not that I am saying anything against Miranda. Indeed I only wish that any of my sisters was half as agreeable as her. She is a dear girl, one of the best, but to find a husband— Well, she has been on the marriage market for a while, has she not?''

''If only Papa had married again after Mama died then we would have had a stepmother to see to such matters, but as it is he insists that I must deal with it in return for settling my debt. What am I to do? How will I ever accomplish it? I shall have to spend the rest of my days struggling to find a husband for Miranda. Oh how I wish I had never sat down at that card-table! Never again will I take part in any game of chance, no, not even beggar my neighbour or spillikins or—''

''There is no need to take on so,'' consoled Peter, fearing that his friend was tottering on the brink of total despair. ''I will give you all the help in my power, and between us we will sort out something. First we must look at the matter practically. Let us work out her attributes—she is well born, educated as befits her station, though she has a deal more sense than most females of my acquaintance."

"And she is good-natured, do not forget that," put in Richard eagerly.

"Indeed, she is the most good-natured creature alive. Now, what is her financial situation?"

"Oh, about three thousand a year, at the moment, though Papa is bound to be as generous as he can manage with her marriage portion."

"Generous enough to double it? Well, that is pretty satisfactory. I am sure there must be plenty of prospective husbands who would be happy to ally themselves to six thousand a year."

"Oh, I say!" protested Richard, suddenly looking anxious. "He must be a decent fellow, you know. Dash it all, Miranda is my sister, and I am deuced fond of her. I would not have her shackled to just any one. The fellow must be—must be a gentleman."

"Of course he must!" declared Peter indignantly. "I am deuced fond of Miranda, too, you know. Do you think I would fob her off with the first Johnny who comes along? No, Miranda will have the best husband we can find for her. I am sure I must know half a dozen fellows, excellent sorts, ripe for marriage, whose only drawbacks are that they are light in the pocket. One of them will surely answer."

"Perhaps we should make a list of the attributes we are seeking in a suitable candidate, just so that there should be no misunderstandings," said Richard, who was feeling a little uneasy at the prospect of these "excellent sorts". "Now, we are both agreed that he should be a gentleman."

"Certain, and then— Oh hullo, is that not Miranda herself coming through the woods?"

The aimless wandering of the two young men had brought them to the boundary between the two estates, and now coming towards them on the Branscombe side was the tall, gangling figure of a young woman.

"So it is." Richard tried unsuccessfully to suppress a sigh. "What has she been up to now?"

The benefits of fresh air and exercise had done nothing whatsoever to improve Miranda Branscombe's appearance, her complexion remained as sallow as ever without even a hint of colour in her cheeks. Moreover, the salt sea wind had removed her bonnet altogether and sent strands of lank mousebrown hair whipping across her face. At the sight of Richard and Peter her solid features lit up with genuine pleasure, and laughter sparkled in her intelligent brown eyes as if at some private joke, but her brother did not notice. All he saw, as she loped towards them, vainly trying to keep at bay a pair of importunate dogs, was that a length of braid hung down from the riding-style jacket that she wore, and that her skirt was bedraggled and besmirched by everything a damp countryside had to offer.

"Oh, our task is hopeless!" he moaned softly, but Peter did not hear him, for he had run on ahead to catch hold of the two battle-scarred dogs that were leaping at Miranda so excitedly.

"What have you in your pocket that is of such interest to these moth-eaten old warriors?" he demanded, laughing.

"I will show you in a minute when Richard gets here. I want to get full enjoyment from the expression on his face when he sees it." Miranda chuckled, her hand protectively covering the large pocket of her jacket.

Richard came puffing up in Peter's wake.

"Really, Miranda, do you not realize that you are all to pieces?" he cried, catching hold of the trailing braid and trying in vain to put it back in place.

Miranda looked at it with scant interest.

"Oh, just let it hang, the dogs will only pull it down again."

"But it is so unsightly. Have you not a pin about you to fix it? And do put your bonnet back on. How can you expect your hair to remain decent in this wind if you let your bonnet dangle so?"

"Now do not get in a state, dear. You know very well that no one takes any notice of me. I am sure our neighbours have far more important things to occupy them than the state of my jacket."

"You are totally wrong, such matters are—Miranda! Your pocket!" Richard's admonition to his sister ended in an alarmed squeak.

"What is wrong with my pocket?" asked Miranda, her eyes dancing.

"It moved!" declared her brother.

"Nonsense! Pockets do not move. Now, the contents might move, but pockets—no, never!"

"Miranda, what have you got in there?" demanded Richard above the increased clamour of the dogs.

"Do you really want to see? Are you sure it will not bite?" she teased.

"Miranda!"

"Very well, but hold on to those two wicked creatures." Carefully she opened her pocket, and both men found themselves looking down at a pair of dark eyes set in a small furry face and topped by ridiculously long ears.

"A leveret, by Harry! What a splendid little fellow," breathed Peter, with a grin.

Richard's reaction was less approving.

"Ugh, a young hare! How can you have it in your pocket? It might—I mean, it could—It is dirty! Where did you get it and what on earth do you propose to do with it?"

"Joe Townson gave it to me. He found the mother dead in a snare and had not the heart to kill the little one."

"If Townson was too sentimental to put an end to it I wonder he did not wish to become its foster-mother," snapped Richard.

"Well, you know the Townsons, their cottage is small and already well filled with children and dogs. I do not think the hare would have stood much chance with them, so I will take it home and rear it. I shall have a nice warm box set by my parlour fire for it to sleep in."

"Miranda, you would not! I mean, I do not know any lady who keeps a tame hare in her boudoir. What will people think? They will consider you to be most eccentric." Richard's face was a picture of despair. Visions of Great-Aunt Evangeline loomed threateningly in his mind, and *she* had only had a tame magpie. Miranda now had a leveret to add to her jackdaw and collection of ill-favoured canines. She was turning Branscombe Hall into a menagerie. It was too much!

Peter Kerswell, however, roared with laughter.

"I should think a pet hare will be extremely jolly," he said. "Think what a diversion it will be in March when it goes mad. I hope you will invite me over to watch the fun."

"Indeed we will," said Richard bitterly. "If by then we have not all been committed to Bedlam. Oh dear, it is just as I feared, Miranda. Look at your skirt. That creature has made a most unpleasant mark."

His sister looked at the ominous stain.

"No, it has not," she said calmly. "That was the Townsons' new baby. I was nursing it."

Richard groaned in mortification while Peter went into fresh roars of laughter.

"Please go home at once and get changed before anyone sees you," begged Richard.

"I certainly will if it distresses you so," Miranda assured him, concerned for her brother's happiness. "Though I must hurry for I promised to go over to old Mr. Cummings. He has been sent the most interesting pamphlet on the iniquities of the Game Laws which I will read to him, his eyes not being up to it, poor dear. Transportation does seem such an exceedingly harsh punishment for merely taking a rabbit to feed one's family, does it not?"

"Miranda, where do you get your gothic ideas!" Richard was shocked to the core.

But Peter was interested. "With a tame hare in your household you will surely find your sympathies much divided. To whom will you give them—to that little fellow in your pocket, to the hordes of folk who will certainly invade your land the minute such a law is repealed or to the sportsman who pays handsomely to rear his own game then finds he has nothing left to shoot?" he asked.

Miranda thought for a moment, then patted the small squirming creature in her pocket.

"My sympathies will always be for those who are most in need of them," she replied.

"Oh, a very politic answer!" laughed Peter. "I see I shall have to consider that remark very carefully."

"Make sure you do," smiled Miranda as she moved away from them. She had tight hold of the two excited dogs who were now tethered together by Peter's neckerchief, a sartorial sacrifice which considerably impressed Richard. He was less impressed by his sister, however.

"We will never find a husband for her," he declared. "She is impossible!"

"Do not face defeat before we have even begun," said Peter, his eyes still twinkling. "There would be many advantages in being wed to Miranda. Life would never be dull, for one thing. Now, what were we discussing just before she interrupted us?"

"We were deciding upon suitable attributes for her future husband, though what qualities can we possibly demand for a female who, besides being plain and having only a modest fortune, keeps a menagerie in her sitting-room, cares not one jot about her appearance, and harbours the most extraordinary radical views?" Richard was determined to regard the situation in its darkest possible light.

"That is the easiest part," replied Peter, producing a stub of pencil and an old bill from his pocket. "The primary quality necessary in any man willing to wed Miranda is obvious."

Then, in his scrawling hand he wrote one word upon the paper—"Tolerance."

CHAPTER TWO

IF RICHARD HAD EXPECTED immediate action from his friend in the matter of finding a husband for Miranda then he was disappointed. Instead of settling down to this urgent task Peter left home that very afternoon in a flurry of hastily packed valises, sparking phaeton wheels and distraught valets. He had gone to Berkshire to complete the purchase of the racing stable, a very frivolous errand in Richard's opinion when they had such a serious matter to tackle.

In Peter's absence he had no option but to begin the search himself. He started by making a list of all the eligible bachelors and widowers in the immediate neighbourhood, but by the time he had eliminated those who were in their dotage, known drunkards or who had already made it plain that they would prefer not to marry Miranda, he was left with one, a middle-aged widower with a large family and small estate.

"Colonel Marks? Never!" his father had exploded when Richard suggested his solitary candidate. "He is such an ill-looking creature! I doubt if he buys a new coat from one year's end to the next. No, I could never call such a shabby fellow 'my son'! Worse still, he might want to address me as 'Papa'. No, he will not do! Think again!"

So poor Richard had drawn a line through Colonel Marks' name, and with a sigh wished fervently that Peter would return. Miranda noted his worried expression.

"Is something troubling you, dear?" she asked. "You have been frowning so all day there is quite a furrow on your brow."

"No, surely not!" Thoroughly alarmed, Richard rushed to the nearest looking-glass and frantically rubbed his forehead. "There, is that better?"

"Much. You look as handsome as ever," his sister assured him. "But you have not answered my question. Is something troubling you? Do you owe money, or have you got yourself into some sort of a scrape? If so, you know you can always count on me for assistance."

"I know I can, but there is no need. Everything is quite all right, I promise you."

Richard felt uncomfortable at his sister's enquiries. She was so sharp where he was concerned, always able to sense when he was upset or in trouble. Ever since they had been children Miranda had eliminated his difficulties for him and soothed away his problems, even though she was a year his junior.

"Are you sure?" Miranda was not convinced. "I am invited to the Crawfords' for tea, but you know I will gladly put aside my arrangements if it will help you."

"But there is nothing wrong. Go ahead and enjoy your tea-party."

"Very well, if you say so. Perhaps I should go now so that I can look in on Jem Price on my way, his roof is leaking again, and something needs to be done."

As Miranda departed a disturbing thought crept into Richard's mind. If Miranda did get married and leave how would he and his father manage, for in her quiet capable way it was she who really controlled the estate, as well as ordering the household. True, the tenants always applied to Sir Henry if they had a problem, but they took care to have a word with Miss Branscombe first if they actually wanted anything done. Richard grew troubled. Did this mean he would have to struggle with matters of accounts and land management? He did not think he could cope; he was not clever, like Miranda.

Feeling very much between the devil and the deep blue sea Richard brooded alone on his difficulties for over a week, unaware that his sister was watching him with silent anxiety. It was a great relief to him when at last Peter was announced.

"My dear fellow, I thought you were gone for ever," he greeted his friend, pumping his hand up and down enthusiastically.

"What a welcome," laughed Peter. "I have only been to Berkshire, you know, not the Antipodes."

"You look very pleased with yourself, wherever you have been," observed Miranda.

"I have good cause," said Peter, stretching out his long legs and accepting the glass of wine that Miranda poured for him. "It is not every day that a man manages to take advantage of a golden opportunity, the best business venture ever."

"As I recall your last venture tripped over its own feet a furlong from home," said Miranda.

"Sheer bad luck. Could happen to anyone." Peter was not to be put down. "But this is a horse of a different colour, if I may use a singularly appropriate metaphor, except that it is not one horse but a whole string of 'em. I have bought a part share in a racing stable."

"That is indeed quite a venture. How many animals have you?" asked Miranda, full of interest.

"Only six at the moment, but we intend to bring over quality yearlings from Ireland and train them. One of my partners will see to that, he can really handle a horse."

"You will need plenty of stable room for such a project."

"Oh we have it. Excellent brick-built housing, will last for ever, and freehold into the bargain. It has taken every penny I could scrape together, but I am well satisfied, for it would have been foolish to join such an enterprise under-capitalized. Of course I do not expect to see any profit for two or three years, maybe even more, but if we concentrate only upon first-class stock I am convinced I will get an excellent return for my investment in the end, as well as the pleasure of owning the horses. Why are you laughing?" For Miranda was grinning all over her face.

"I was thinking how surprised your father would be to hear you talking in such a business-like manner. Do you know, you sounded exactly like him."

"Do not say that! My Old Gentleman would be horrified. He considers me to be a truly shatter-brained fellow."

"Sir John would be even more horrified to hear you calling him your Old Gentleman. But the truth remains, you grow more like him each day, the only difference being that where he spends his intelligence in matters of serious finance you spend yours upon horse racing. I truly hope the agreement for this stable of yours was properly drawn up."

"Of course it was. Do you take me for a ninny? I consulted Meredith, we have done business with him for years, and he saw to it that everything was aboveboard and sewn up tight and legal. A good lawyer is always worth his fee." Then Peter, too, started to laugh. "You are right, Miranda, I do begin to sound like my Old Gentleman. It must be being a man of affairs that does it."

Richard had been listening to this conversation with ill-concealed impatience. Not only did he find the subject boring, he was most eager to speak to Peter on matters far more vital than agreements of sale and freeholds of land.

"All this talk of horses had put me in the mood for a good gallop," he declared, with blatantly false heartiness.

"Well, I am agreeable if Miranda will excuse us," said Peter, who guessed the reason for his friend's sudden need for activity.

But Miranda was not taken in by her brother's desire for the open air.

"I will excuse you gladly—just as soon as I find out what you two are up to," she said.

At this Richard jumped guiltily.

"Whatever do you mean?" he stammered. Peter, on the other hand, was far more self-possessed.

"Are you developing a suspicious mind, Miranda?" he asked calmly. "Why should we be up to something? We have not seen each other for near enough a week."

"If you would have a fellow conspirator you should choose someone other than Richard, he has no talent for dissembling," she replied. "All the time you have been away he has been filled with anxiety, then the minute you get back he greets you like a long-lost brother, and for this last half-hour he has scarcely been able to sit still while we conversed. You two are up to something, I know it."

Again Peter laughed and tapped Miranda playfully on the nose.

"Well, my inquisitive lady, you will just have to curb your curiosity for a while. However, I promise that you will know all about it presently." And with that he bustled an agitated Richard out of the room.

"Peter, I have had a most capital notion," exclaimed Richard as soon as they were out of earshot.

"You have? Congratulations, my friend."

"Oh, do stop ribbing! I am serious. This matter of finding a husband for Miranda has vexed me sorely. I am worn to the bone with worry over it, but it has occurred to me that help might be at hand. Could we not ask Lady Kerswell for assistance? After all, she must be regarded as something of an expert, having married off every one of your sisters most creditably."

Peter, however, was not enthusiastic.

"As I remember it Mama had very little to do with getting rid of my sisters, other than writing guest lists and continually badgering the Old Gentleman for more money for bride clothes. The girls managed all the rest themselves. Once they decided upon a suitable male the poor fellow was lured and landed like a stunned salmon before he knew anything was amiss. Sophia, for example, had made up her mind to have poor Bagshaw within a sennight of meeting him, and after that he did not stand a chance. No, I do not consider that we need involve Mama, except as a last resort. Besides, I have already found an excellent candidate for Miranda's hand."

"You have?" cried Richard, astounded. "Then why did you not say so earlier?"

Peter looked puzzled.

"Because I had other matters on my mind. My share in the stable—"

"Yes, yes," interrupted Richard, regretting that his friend did not share his own single-mindedness. "Who is he? Do I know him? Is he of good family?"

"Which question shall I answer first?" asked Peter, prevaricating wickedly. "Ouch! All right! Stop beating me and I will tell you. Firstly his name is Arnold Denley, and I doubt if you have his acquaintance, he is not one for going out into society much. He is a gentleman of the purest character, never having had the stamina to be anything else. A bachelor, aged about thirty, with a good income and the sort of impeccable pedigree which comes from kinship with the Kerswells. He is a second cousin thrice removed or a third cousin twice removed, I forget which. Whatever his relationship it is high time he was married."

"He sounds perfect," declared Richard, too delighted to suspect any flaws in this paragon.

"Yes, does he not? You will have the chance to look him over next week, for he is coming to visit us. We must organize things so that he and Miranda will discover their mutual attraction."

"What if they do not form an attachment?"

"We will give them no option. The way we will execute matters there will be a betrothal within the month. Such a vital affair is far too important to be left simply to them. True love will need a firm, helping hand."

Such resolve suggested that Peter already had some strategy in mind, which was very comforting, for Richard's brain had little aptitude for plotting, but twenty years of past, frequently painful, experience had taught him that Peter's plans needed to be approached with caution.

"How can you be so sure? Is your cousin on the look-out for a wife?"

"Cousin Denley does not yet know that what he needs most in this world is a wife. It will be up to us to persuade him. So far his nerves have never been strong enough to withstand the rigours of matrimony—he fancies himself to be a martyr to nerves, I understand. They are the reason why he has never before visited us, the prospect of all the Kerswells at home together was a bit much for him. I suppose he feels he can cope with just the parents and me. I only hope he has judged aright. I cannot help feeling that he is in ignorance of the newer springs on the Kerswell family tree. There's Maria's tribe, and Arabella's three boys, and Lucy's family, and Lizzie's clutch—to mention only those within immediate visiting distance. They all fight like the devil and cause no end of a rumpus. Jolly little souls, the lot of them, and tremendous fun, but a bit wearing if one's nerves are tender, I should imagine."

Richard, who found Peter's innumerable nephews and nieces hard going at the best of times, had to agree. He was also beginning to harbour the faintest of misgivings about Mr. Arnold Denley.

"He is all right, I suppose? Your Cousin Denley I mean."

"All right? Of course he is. He is not dipped in the head, if that is what you are hinting at, though he is rather whey-faced and inclined to be puny. No, apart from his nerves he enjoys tremendous ill health—he should suit Miranda admirably. You know what she is like about looking after folks, well, she will have a husband who will lap up every bit of fussing and cosseting she cares to offer."

Richard brightened at this.

"Yes, it might work. Nanny Hart is sure to go with Miranda once she is married, and there is nothing Nanny likes better than a good invalid."

"There, the three of them will be very happy, I am sure."

His misgivings totally dispelled, Richard awaited Mr. Denley's arrival with eager anticipation. Miranda, ever sensitive to her brother's moods, noticed that his worried frown had been superseded by an air of excitement. This change would have pleased her if she had not also noted a sparkle of suppressed mischief in Peter Kerswell's green eyes.

"There is no doubt about it," she told herself. "The two of them are definitely up to something."

It was fortunate that she was totally unaware their plotting involved herself, or she would not have gone about her activities with her usual good humour.

Miranda knew very well that she was plain. How could she help it when for most of her three-and-twenty years she had been the recipient of pitying glances? Even Nanny Hart, her old nurse, who was partial to a fault where her Miss Miranda was concerned, had long since given up uttering such pieces of hopeful wisdom as "Plain in the cradle, a beauty at the table." Miranda had been "at the table" for years with no improvement at all. Apart from the fact that her plainness distressed her father and at times embarrassed Richard she did not mind too much. It had its compensations. Since she was a threat to no female and had a handsome, eligible brother, not to say an equally handsome and eligible father, she was welcome everywhere. As a result her circle of friends was wide, comparable with her interests, which stretched far beyond the bounds required of a young lady of society. But Miranda Branscombe was so ill-looking what did it signify if she concerned herself with eccentric subjects? The general goings-on in Europe, the study of incomprehensible and unpleasant creatures that lurked at the bottom of ponds, the basic principles of the steam engine—these were just some of the subjects encompassed by Miranda's quick and eager brain. If Sir Henry Branscombe had really known the full depth and extent of her enquiries he would have been considerably more agitated than he was already.

In turn Miranda would have been surprised to learn how much her father's thoughts dwelt upon getting her married. For herself she had long ago dispelled matrimony to the realms of impossible dreams. She knew that she was too plain for anyone to contemplate her for a wife, so why torment herself striving for the unattainable? Instead she had her friends, her many interests, the estate and the house to attend to. She was busy and she was happy.

Miranda could not have guessed that when she accepted an invitation to dine at New Park it would be to meet a possible husband, which was why she alone of the Branscombe family dressed for the occasion with equanimity. Her brother was in a dither of nerves about the evening, and her father, who had been quietly informed about the arrival of Mr. Arnold Denley and his possible future influence upon the Branscombe household, became in such an agitated state that he ruined ten cravats before he was even tolerably satisfied with his appearance. After all, he might be about to meet his future son-in-law, so it was imperative that he make a good impression.

"Peter says to simply act normally this evening and to leave all the cupid's dart business to him," Richard had whispered conspiratorially in Sir Henry's ear.

Sir Henry had readily agreed. Like his son, in everything other than sartorial affairs, he was only too pleased to leave matters in someone else's hands.

Ushered into the splendid *salon* at New Park the Branscombes got their first view of Arnold Denley. Sir Henry noted that he was wearing the latest style of Wellington frock-coat, splendidly tailored in blue velvet, and also perfectly fitting pantaloon trousers in the style made famous by the unfortunate Mr. Brummel. Added to which he sported a perfectly arranged neckpiece *à la Byron*. Which immediately aroused Sir Henry's admiration. Yes, he would not be ashamed to be seen with such a son-in-law.

Richard's first impressions were less enthusiastic, particularly when he noted that Mr. Denley was nearly two feet shorter than his future bride. The fellow might be all that Peter said he was, but observing the dull eyes and the languid demeanour of this Denley, Richard was convinced that they would have their work cut out bringing him up to scratch.

Miranda, blissfully unaware that she was meeting her destiny, merely saw a slight, pale little man who looked sickly, and she felt sorry for him.

Mr. Denley set his seal upon the conversation at the earliest opportunity, the moment they sat down to dine.

"It is most kind of my cousins, dear Sir John and Lady Kerswell, to have me as their guest," he began in a high carrying tone. "I would not have them put out for my sake, not for the world, therefore I have warned them not to be in the least surprised if one morning they find me a lifeless corpse in bed, my soul having fled to Elysian Fields."

The convivial chatter came to an astonished halt the length and breadth of the table as startled eyes stared in Mr. Denley's direction, Miranda, who by some curious chance was sitting at his right hand, recovered her composure first.

"Is such a melancholy occurrence likely to happen, sir?" she asked politely.

"Oh, I expect it daily, even hourly. With a constitution as frail as mine one must be ever ready for the hand of the Final Reaper. Why, at any moment I might fall stone-dead, even right now across this very table, who can tell?" Mr. Denley sounded remarkably cheerful at the prospect, but his observations were followed by a unanimous clatter as his fellow-guests returned their forks to their plates, their appetites flown. Again it was Miranda who somehow managed to appear unperturbed.

"I beg you will do no such thing, sir," she replied with commendable calm. "Lady Kerswell is always most concerned for her guests' welfare, and I know it would distress her sorely for you to depart so prematurely before you have finished your dinner."

"That is very true, Miss Branscombe, a most wise thought." Mr. Denley nodded earnestly, then he turned and beamed at his hostess. "Out of consideration to you, my dear Lady Kerswell, I shall endeavour to remain within this mortal coil for as long as possible, and certainly until dinner is at an end."

Reassured by this statement the Kerswells and their guests resumed their dining, though their butler, observing a certain lack of enthusiasm for food which had suddenly descended, tactfully ensured that all portions were a deal smaller than usual.

Having temporarily abandoned his demise as a source of conversation, Mr. Denley turned to the reasons for its imminence, and a torrent of high-voiced hypochondria flooded from his lips, mainly into the unfortunate ears of Miranda.

"See that? They're getting on splendidly together," whispered Peter to Richard as the ladies left them after the meal. Being irritated by cigar smoke and too dyspeptic for port Arnold Denley had accompanied them, much wrapped in shawls in case an errant draught might creep out of the mild spring evening and blow on him. What had encouraged Peter was the fact that he had been supported by a footman on one side and on the other by Miranda, as the most robust of the ladies. There were six shallow steps to be negotiated *en route* to the withdrawing-room, and Denley was afraid of overexerting himself.

"Peter, are you convinced that this is a good idea?" After only a few hours in Denley's company Richard was harbouring some serious doubts about the alliance.

"Convinced? Of course I'm convinced. They are ideal for each other." Peter's face was a mask of innocence.

"How can you say that? Miranda is head and shoulders bigger than he is. And dash it all, he is a terrible bore!"

"A trifle self-centred, I will admit," replied Peter, ignoring the fact that he had suppressed so many yawns his eyes were streaming. "But what alternative is there?"

Richard was forced to admit that alternatives were few. He muttered, "I only hope they do not come visiting us much once they are married. Miranda can come as often as she pleases, but your Cousin Denley—"

As they returned to Branscombe Hall later that night Richard ventured to sound out his sister's opinion of their new acquaintance.

"A pleasant enough gentleman," she replied. "How sad that he has only his own ailments with which to concern himself. I fancy poor Lady Kerswell must find him something of a trial, so we must do everything we can to help her keep him entertained."

Not a very lover-like speech, but full of sympathy. Richard closed his mind to the fact that Miranda would have been just as sympathetic towards the meanest inmate of the local poor-house. He preferred to keep his thoughts on more positive lines. Miranda was quite prepared to meet Denley again. That could only be a good sign. The rest would be up to Peter's organizing abilities.

To give Peter his due he worked unceasingly in his rôle of latter-day Cupid. It was entirely due to his efforts that Miranda always sat next to Denley at meals, was always in the same carriage when they went on expeditions, and at the same table when fours were made up for whist. Miranda had no head for cards, but with Arnold Denley this did not matter for he could never take his mind off his own delicious state of ill health long enough to remember what was trumps. At the end of three weeks Peter was worn out with plotting and scheming, and so much of Cousin

Denley's company had frayed his normally cheery temper. In spite of his airy assurances to Richard he was beginning to feel sorry for Miranda having to spend the rest of her life with such a fellow. For himself he would have much preferred to be incarcerated with every one of his sisters' progeny at their noisy, quarrelsome worst.

Between the Branscombes, *père et fils*, it had become the regular assumption that Miranda would marry Arnold Denley, even if such a matter had to remain unspoken to others. They managed to persuade themselves that the match was a foregone conclusion, for was he not the most suitable spouse they could hope for? The little snags of peevishness and boredom were regarded as merely the normal hazards of matrimony. So set did they become in their complacency that it came as quite a shock to realize that Mr. Denley's visit had only a few more days to run and that he had still not made an offer.

"What is to be done? He leaves on Thursday and then he will be lost to us," demanded Richard anxiously.

"For my part I will not be sorry." Peter was looking a trifle green about the gills. "All through breakfast he regaled me with an epic regarding the activities of his liver, no detail omitted, no process unexplained. Put me completely off my fodder! I tell you, Richard, I am having serious doubts about this match. Miranda is a dear girl, it seems a shame to shackle her to Cousin Denley."

"Oh, but it is necessary!" Panic made Richard's voice sharp at this sudden change of mind. "We must marry her off. The matter grows more urgent. She is truly becoming more like Great-Aunt Evangeline with every day that passes. That tame jackdaw of hers has taken to flying about the house, attacking the maids. The place is in an uproar, I tell you, and all Miranda does is laugh. Denley must marry her!"

Peter decided that this hectic incident bore little relation to the version he had already heard from Miranda, in which her bird had escaped once and alighted upon a housemaid, who, far from suffering an attack of hysterics, had fed it upon currants soaked in wine, so founding a lasting friendship. However, he did recognize that Miranda needed a husband. Intelligent and capable as she was, the modern world of 1820 was no place for an unmarried lady. Arnold Denley would have to do.

At that moment Peter suffered one of the flashes of inspiration that his family and friends had come to dread.

"Fear not, my dear fellow," he declared with a dramatic flourish. "All shall be accomplished."

"But how?"

"Mama has organized one more function for our cousin, a *fête champêtre*, to be held tomorrow. You all have invitations, I know, because I delivered them myself. Tomorrow it shall be when Cousin Denley goes down on his knees—if the grass ain't wet—and begs for Miranda's hand."

"How can you be sure?"

"The scene will be perfect—the dappled shade of the trees, the swans skimming serenely over the lake, and balmy breezes. Cousin Denley will not be able to help but propose, though he might need just a touch of assistance from the pair of us. Now listen to my plan—"

Richard did listen. At first with hopeful optimism, but then with growing horror.

"I could never do that! Never! Never!" he declared when Peter had finished.

Peter put a hand upon his shoulder.

"Courage, my friend," he said gravely. "Hard times need hard measures. Think only of Miranda's future. Can you fail her at such a vital moment?"

"No, I suppose not. Very well. I will do as you say," replied Richard, but he spoke without any enthusiasm at all.

CHAPTER THREE

LADY KERSWELL'S *fête champêtre* had all the ingredients necessary to be an unqualified success; the food and wine were excellent, the day was pleasantly warm, and it was early enough in the year for such an alfresco event to be a novelty. Sweet music, from a band of musicians tucked away in the gazebo, wafted over the carefully improved grounds of New Park. The guests strolled about the greensward, delighted to be freed from the confines of winter, and some of the younger, livelier element were even more delighted to find that that freedom encompassed some splendidly conceived shrubberies, ideal for carrying out flirtations.

"It is a great pity that we cannot just let nature take its course," remarked Richard, watching one high-spirited young lady emerge from a stout clump of ilex bushes pursued by a scarlet-coated army officer. "Everyone else seems to be managing their love-life most satisfactorily, so why cannot Miranda and Denley?"

"Ah, but we are concerned with matrimony, not love," observed Peter sagely.

"True. It does make a difference."

"It certainly does. Now, are you quite sure that you know your part?"

"I should do. I paced my bedchamber all last night working out what I was to say. I must look downright haggard this morning, my eyes are all red and puffy. I am not fit to be seen."

For once Peter had no reassurance to give concerning his friend's appearance. Richard did look haggard.

"It does not matter what you look like so long as you remember what to do. I have got the messages organized, now it is just a matter of timing. Miranda must get there before Cousin Denley. Oh look! What devilish luck! They are together at this moment. All month I have worn myself to a standstill trying to get them into each other's company, and the one occasion when we want them apart they are chatting like the veriest bosom bows."

"They do seem to enjoy being together," pointed out Richard. "You do not think that there is any chance— I mean, would it not be a caper if Denley proposed off his own bat, without any help from us?"

"Do not even consider it. If Cousin Denley is running true to form then he is holding forth on one or other of his ailments. Let me see, he has already discussed his liver, his lungs, his bladder, and his heart— all at meal-times, I might add—so all that is left of his lights must be his kidneys. I will wager a gold 'un that the subject of his conversation is his kidneys."

"Taken!" accepted Richard morosely.

As it happened he would have won the wager if there had been any method of proving the matter. Arnold was not discussing his health at all but his plans for quitting this life in a true and fitting manner.

"Dear Rector Brownjohn has been most obliging and constructive in helping to decide my funeral service. Many an hour we have sat together pondering on the most appropriate form. One likes to have such matters properly organized, does not one? The Dean of Bath and Wells has agreed to give the funeral oration, and I was bold enough to send him a few notes for his guidance—my suffering on this earth, borne with such fortitude—that sort of thing. He was most grateful, I can tell you. He said he had never before had such assistance from the recipient of his ministrations. I have had the full order of service specially printed and bound in calf—black calf of course—with gold lettering, and I carry it everywhere with me. It is my favourite reading, and such a comfort. I wonder if you would be kind enough to adjust my shawl higher on my neck? The wind has changed direction, I swear it has."

Suppressing a sigh Miranda did as she was asked, even though there was scarcely enough breeze to ruffle the surface of the lake. She dearly would have loved to have escaped from the tedium of Mr. Denley's monologue, but that would have left the poor little man alone, the entire neighbourhood having already learnt the art of avoiding him with the resemblance of utmost civility.

Miranda had two reasons for wishing herself free from Mr. Denley's funereal conversation on that delightful afternoon, quite apart from the excruciating boredom she was suffering. The first was her anxiety over her brother and Peter. They were up to something, and no amount of protestations to the contrary would persuade her otherwise. The conspiratorial air of the pair of them, coupled with a lifetime's experience, made her very wary. Anyone observing them strolling across the lawn would have regarded them as simply two elegant young Society gentlemen, but Miranda knew better. Beneath the impeccable tailoring there lurked a pair of mischievous, schoolboy hearts, at least in Peter's case, and Richard usually followed his friend. Miranda knew that they were quite capable of adding liver salts to the punch or introducing live frogs beneath the pastry crusts of the raised pies, and she was determined to keep an eye on them in the hope of preventing possible disaster.

Her other reason for wishing to escape from Arnold Denley's recitation was more personal. A widowed lady, a Mrs. Parkinson, had come to reside in the district, and had already become known for her very radical views, views which Miranda found most interesting. Mrs. Parkinson was to be at the *fête champêtre* and had promised to pass on to Miranda some pamphlets about Mr. Robert Owen's experiments in constructing rural villages that were positively Utopian in their concept. There had to be a certain amount of subterfuge about the transaction because it was unlikely that Sir Henry would approve of his daughter's new friend. Miranda had no wish to deceive her father, merely to save him pain, for she was aware that it was not the humanitarian ideals of wishing to see workers properly housed which would distress him. How could they, when he never gave such notions a thought? No, it would be the knowledge that his daughter was interested in so outlandish a matter. Therefore Miranda now watched covertly for the arrival of Mrs. Parkinson.

However, it was not the lady who arrived, but Mr. Denley's manservant, who announced firmly that it was time for his master's next dose of physic. He then bore the invalid away to a place of privacy for the operation. Miranda received the arrival of the servant with much the same relief as the imprisoned Richard the Lionheart must have felt upon hearing the voice of Blondel. She stood up, shook out her skirts and made her escape.

It was some time later that a footman handed her a note. She read:

> *My dear Miss B.,*
> *Pray meet me in the boat-house. I beg you wait until I come, it is a matter of great delicacy.*
> *Your obedient servant,*

The initials at the end were ill-formed and rather smudged, so that they could have been almost any letters. However, after some scrutiny, Miranda decided that they must be H.P. for Hester Parkinson. She gave a little smile. That lady's views were sincerely held but often tinged with high drama.

Or perhaps I overemphasized the need for discretion when she gives me the pamphlets, decided Miranda charitably. Whatever the reason I had best go to the boat-house and find out.

The boat-house, situated beside the lake at New Park, was a ramshackle wooden building, contrasting strangely with the luxurious grandeur of the rest of the estate. The reason was a difference of opinion between Sir John and his wife. As Sir John put it, "Having spent a nabob's ransom on the improvements to the park I want an edifice here worthy of my outlay, a Greek temple, perhaps, with one or two imported marble goddesses."

"What we really require, my love," Lady Kerswell always replied with equal determination, "is a pretty summer-house with wide steps down to the water, where the children can play when they come to visit us—properly supervised, of course."

As a result of this impasse it looked as though the boat-house would remain in its dilapidated state until Nature finally had its way and it fell down altogether.

Confident that this collapse was not imminent, Miranda made her way there, pushed open the door and sat down in its spider-infested interior to await her friend.

"Well, there goes Miranda," whispered Peter, from the cover of a convenient clump of willows. "Cousin Denley should not keep us long."

"Perhaps he will not come at all," suggested Richard. There was a hopefulness in his voice that hinted that Mr. Denley's non-appearance would not disappoint him greatly.

"He will come, never fear," replied Peter, dashing all Richard's expectations. "I sent him a note he could not refuse. It said, 'The cure for all your ills awaits you in the old boat-house. Do not delay, but be sure to come alone.'"

Richard heaved a big sigh.

"You are right. Denley would never turn down the chance to acquire yet another cure-all. He is not to know that the only remedy awaiting him is marriage to Miranda."

"And you do not consider marriage to be the cure for everything? Come, Richard, I never thought you to be a cynic. No, the more I think of our scheme the more convinced I am that it is to everyone's advantage. Miranda will have the husband she needs, you will have fulfilled your obligation to your father, and as for Cousin Denley, he will benefit most of all. Marriage to Miranda will be the making of him, you mark my words."

Peter's enthusiasm would have been more encouraging if Richard had not detected a false heartiness beneath it. Knowledge that his friend was having second thoughts increased his own misgivings.

"You do not believe that, not truly," he cried. "Let us abandon the whole thing and return to the party before matters go any further. Your plan will not work. It will be a total disaster and there will be the devil to pay afterwards. Besides, this place is uncommon boggy, and my feet are getting deuced wet. Let us go immediately."

As he turned Peter detained him with a firm hand on his shoulder.

"Do not be faint-hearted now. Things are going so well. You will not thank me for it if I let you run away at this moment. As your friend I insist that you stay. It is our last chance with Cousin Denley. We cannot let him slip from our clutches. Besides, here he comes now. You cannot go without being seen."

Reluctantly Richard allowed himself to be dragged back into the cover of the willows, while, a few yards away, Mr. Denley approached the boat-house, his pale thin face alight with curiosity and anticipation.

"Ahem! Coo-ee!" Arnold Denley called softly when he was a short distance from the boat-house door. "Coo-eee, is anyone there?"

From her seat inside Miranda restrained a groan; Mr. Denley, of all people! How was she going to escape him this time? She did consider remaining silent, but decided against it. If he was to come upon her unexpectedly he would quite likely die of fright.

"It is I, Mr. Denley," she replied.

"Ah, Miss Branscombe, so you are to be the author of my relief," answered Arnold Denley, happy to have approached his goal, though a little puzzled by the subterfuge employed. Why could not Miss Branscombe have spoken when they were having such a comfortable coze not half an hour since?

"I beg your pardon, Mr. Denley?" Miranda's bewilderment matched his own.

"Do you not understand? I have come in reply to your letter," began Denley, stepping into the boathouse. He had no chance to say more for the door suddenly slammed behind him, shutting out all the light, but not before he had glimpsed cobweb-festooned rafters with hairy spiders ready to drop upon him, and dusty corners filled with nasty scuttling creatures prepared to pounce. Mr. Denley's reaction was immediate. He let out a shriek of terror, and swooned into Miranda's arms.

"Can we let them out now?" Richard asked miserably from the clump of willows. Inside his hessian boots his feet were decidedly cold and wet, and as for the boots themselves, they were past all redemption.

"Twenty minutes we agreed to give them," answered Peter, his eyes on his fob-watch.

"It must be that by now."

"It is scarce five minutes. If you are so weary with waiting why do you not sit down?"

Richard looked at the muddy ground and shuddered. Ruining his hessians was bad enough without adding a pair of excellent cream jersey inexpressibles to the disasters of the day.

"I prefer to stand," he said, trying to ignore the fact that he was sinking deeper and deeper into the mud.

He had to stand for a long time, so long, in fact, that he was convinced that Peter's watch had stopped. His heart was pounding with nervousness, and he was convinced that he would botch the whole thing.

"Time to go, old fellow." Peter put his watch away. "Now, remember, stroll nonchalantly to the boat-house as though you had no idea what to expect, open the door, then play the enraged brother for all you are worth. Bringing down the grey hairs of your poor old father, that sort of thing."

"Oh, I do not think I had better say that. Papa would be most put out. Besides, his hair is not grey, more a delicate shade of silver."

"Do it which way you please, only move!" insisted Peter, pulling his friend from the mud. In truth he, too, would be glad when this business was over. He was not afraid it would fail, it was success that he dreaded, and the future life to which poor Miranda would be condemned.

The pair of them walked slowly towards the boat-house, their heads bent as though in conversation, though neither of them could think of a thing to say. The boat-house was eerily silent as they approached, and the two friends looked at each other in some alarm.

"Should there not be some noise? Talking or cries for help?" whispered Richard.

"Not necessarily. Oh, use your imagination, a man and a young lady alone together."

Richard's imagination, never particularly strong, withered and died completely when forced to concentrate upon a scene in which Miranda was in the fond embrace of Arnold Denley.

"I— I think I had better get on with it," he said.

Taking hold of the key he unlocked the door and flung it open, crying, in a voice raised several octaves by sheer nerves, "Egad, sir, what is this I find?"

The scene was not at all what he had envisaged. Arnold Denley, his face pale green and perspiring, lay semiconscious, supported by Miranda. Nor were the latter's reactions at all appropriate to a young lady caught in a compromising situation with a gentleman.

"You took your time in coming," she said coldly. "Fetch Peter from wherever he is skulking and lift poor Mr. Denley out into the fresh air. He is unwell."

"You were expecting us?" Richard stared at her.

"Who else would have played such a stupid trick? Now, fetch Peter immediately or I shall lift Mr. Denley myself."

This horrifying threat, and the knowledge that his sister was quite capable of carrying it out, spurred Richard to do as he was told. One look at his face was enough to tell Peter that their plan had failed. Sheepishly the tall young man emerged from this hiding-place and faced Miranda's stony glare.

"Move him gently, and put him in the shade. No, on the other side of the bushes. I am sure the poor man has no wish to be a peep-show for the whole neighbourhood. There, there, Mr. Denley, you are out in the fresh air now. Your ordeal is over. You will feel better by and by."

Peter and Richard watched as she ministered to the prone figure, shuffling their feet awkwardly, longing to make their escape, yet knowing that they had to stay.

"Is—is he all right?" asked Peter, at length.

"He is looking better, well enough to be taken back to the house. You two will have to carry him, for I assume that you will want matters to be as discreet as possible." Miranda gave the pair of them a stern look. Richard's eyes filled with tears, and even Peter's face turned red to be so silently reproved by one who normally gave only approbation.

"Yes, I think we can get him back with as little fuss as possible," replied Peter. The two young men took up their slight burden and began to move towards the house.

"When you have seen Mr. Denley to his room and being well cared for I suggest that you both return here. I have a strange desire for a second secluded rendezvous at this boat-house, so I trust that neither of you will disappoint me."

"Oh no, Miranda," replied the pair of them obediently.

Half an hour later they stood before her once more, Arnold Denley having been delivered into the care of his manservant. A very hang-dog couple they looked too, with Richard anguished beneath the twin burdens of guilt and failure and Peter bracing himself for the box on the ear which would surely have followed if Miranda had been one of his own sisters. Instead, the lady observed them calmly out of steady brown eyes.

"Tell me, what possessed you to try and make a match of it between Mr. Denley and myself?" she asked.

Two pairs of eyes stared at her in surprise.

"A match between you and Denley? What stuff!" Richard tried to bluster his way out of difficulties, but Peter shook his head.

"You are a sharp one, Miranda," he said. "How did you guess?"

"I would have been a veritable ninny not to have seen through your ploy. I wondered why I seemed to be for ever in that poor little man's company, and it was obvious that you two were scheming. Today's venture made it a certainty. Now all I need to know is why?"

"We had to find a husband for you," Richard said, carefully avoiding his sister's eyes.

"Had to? Why the urgency? I know Papa used to be in a stew about my lack of suitors, but I thought he had given up. And what has brought you two into the hunt?"

"I promised Papa I would find you a husband if he would repay a debt for me. He is getting into a state about you because of your jackdaw and the hare and things, just like Great-Aunt Evangeline, and you know what she was like, and Peter joined in because I owed the money to him, and besides I did not know where to start and he is so good with ideas and Denley was the best we could come up with but he goes home soon so we had to think up something in a hurry." Richard rattled out the words at a great rate.

Peter gave a groan and closed his eyes. Honesty might be the best policy, but his friend had gone to extremes. Silently he prayed that Miranda had experienced difficulty in interpreting the gabbled speech.

No one spoke in the boat-house. Only the buzzing of a solitary bluebottle and the far-off voices of the *fête champêtre* broke the stillness.

"I presume it was Papa's idea that you had to find me a husband?" Miranda spoke at last.

"Yes."

"And this afternoon's extraordinary episode was devised by Peter?"

"Yes."

Again there was silence, and again Peter steeled himself for the storm which must surely follow. He tried to imagine what would have happened if he had played such a trick on one of his sisters, and quailed at the very thought.

But no outburst came from Miranda. Instead she said very quietly, "You should both be ashamed of yourselves. Did it never occur to you what such a prank might do to one of Mr. Denley's nervous disposition? Whether he is truly delicate or whether he merely fancies himself to be so does not matter. What does matter is that he suffered most dreadfully at being enclosed in a confined space. I am inured to your mad escapades, but he is not. The results might have been most serious, and I confess that I am surprised at the pair of you, that you should have shown such thoughtlessness.''

It was a very mildly delivered speech, with none of the anger and hysterical outbursts which might reasonably have been expected, yet the very gentleness of its reproof was enough to make both young men thoroughly chastened, and Peter, for one, heartily wished that the floor would open and swallow him up.

"We are very sorry, Miranda, truly we are, eh, Richard?" he said humbly, but Richard could only nod and twist his handkerchief in his fingers.

"You should apologize to Mr. Denley, he suffered the hurt," said Miranda. "Now let us consider the subject of my marriage. I must confess that I am not at all pleased to have such a matter left in your hands, for, as you have already proved most forcibly, you are likely to make a sorry mess of it. However, you have given your word to get me wed, have you not, Richard, and I cannot see how we can get round it. Poor Papa, he must be very anxious to have extracted such a promise from you. For myself, I would not mind growing to be more like Great-Aunt Evangeline, she sounds a lot more interesting than most of our ancestors, but of course such a trait would upset Papa most dreadfully. Oh dear, I do feel responsible for getting you into such a situation, for if I were not the plainest, most awkward creature imaginable this would never have happened. Now you are honour bound to find me a husband, whether either of us likes it or not. I suppose the only solution is for me to cooperate as best I can before you frighten some other unsuspecting gentleman half to death."

"You mean you would like to get married?" Richard stared at her.

"Not in particular, but seemingly I must, to release you from the promise you gave to Papa. Also, I can see that Papa will be in a fret until I find a husband. Yes, I must assist you as much as possible, else you will never have any peace."

"Miranda, you are the dearest girl who ever lived," cried Richard.

"Hear, hear!" agreed Peter, swinging her completely off her feet, a show of high spirits that would certainly have earned him a second box on the ear from any of his female relatives.

"But mind," warned Miranda as, flushed and breathless, she regained her balance, "no more Mr. Denleys if you please. I know he is your kinsman, Peter, and I have no wish to offend you, but I fear I do find him a trifle wearing on the patience."

"Agreed!" shouted the gentlemen in unison.

One person who heartily endorsed Miranda's view of Arnold Denley was Sir John Kerswell, and his reaction to the news that Mr. Denley was to spend another week under his roof was loud in the extreme.

"A whole week? It cannot be borne! I shall leave home myself!" he roared when his wife imparted the information at breakfast.

"He is poorly, my dear. We cannot turn the unfortunate creature out from his sick-bed," said Lady Kerswell. She had the implacable calm common to mothers who have successfully reared large families and still retained their sanity, but even she had to admit that this latest piece of news had come perilously close to oversetting her.

"We could try! What brought on this sudden attack of the vapours?"

"I could not get to the bottom of it quite. Some hum about having been locked in the boat-house with Miranda Branscombe."

"With Miranda?" Sir John lowered the forkful of devilled kidney that had almost reached his lips. "With Miranda? You do not think that—but she is up here and he is down there." He indicated their relative heights with his fork.

"I agree, my dear, not a match that readily springs to mind."

"It all sounds havey-cavey to me. That boy of yours is at the bottom of it, I would bet my last ha'penny on it."

"Why is Peter always my boy if he has done something wrong, never yours?" observed Lady Kerswell without rancour.

"He is no son of mine, that harum-scarum rascal!"

"You have left it a little late to accuse me of introducing a cuckoo into your nest. Besides, it will not wash. He is the image of you in looks as well as ways. You were just as much an imp of Satan when you were his age. Why else do you think I had you?"

"Stuff!" Sir John took refuge behind his copy of *The Times* only to emerge immediately. "The fact remains that Peter's antics have forced Cousin Denley's company upon us for another week, and it will be a long time before I forgive the boy for that. I have half a mind to cut him out of my will. For once I thank heaven that the Season is almost upon us and we will be packing our bags for London in a few days. It is still a mystery why your son should suddenly wish to promote an alliance between Miranda and little Denley, though. Miranda and Denley!" And he hastily put up his *Times* to mask his chuckles.

Upstairs, in his darkened bedchamber, Arnold Denley lay with a vinegar cloth on his head, hartshorn and smelling salts within easy reach, and his calf-bound copy of the funeral service by his bedside in case these minutes might be his last. From time to time Denley permitted himself a groan, just to prove that such a critical moment had not yet come. In his mind he dwelt on his dark and terrible adventure in the boat-house. Without doubt it was the most dreadful episode in his life, and how he was alive to tell the tale—or at least think about it—he did not know. If it had not been for the kindness of Miss Branscombe he was convinced that he would have expired. Miss Branscombe! Not all of the events in the boat-house had been appalling. It had been a long time since a feminine hand had stroked his brow so gently, not since his dear mama had gone to a Better World. Yes, Miss Branscombe had been truly wonderful. Denley recalled how calm she had been, loosening his neck-cloth for him, talking to him so softly about the generous flow of air coming through the cracks, and how they were sure to be rescued shortly—all so reassuring. Above all, she had been really concerned for him. Well provided with servants as he was, Denley was only too well aware of how he lacked someone to care for him. Someone like a mother or a wife. His mama was irreplaceable—but a wife? Denley had never seriously considered matrimony before, it involved too much of having other people rely upon him, looking to him for help and support. No, his health was not up to such responsibilities, but to have a wife that he could lean on—someone like Miranda Branscombe, for instance? How capable she had been, knowing just how to give the right amount of reassurance, and knowing, too, how to administer smelling salts properly. It was surprising how few people had the right knack with smelling salts—not too far away so as to be ineffective, nor so close as to burn the nose. No, Miss

Branscombe had been just right. True, she had not had a smelling bottle of her own, but that was a very minor fault which slow and patient training could soon rectify. Yes, Miss Branscombe had been very, very kind.

Arnold Denley lay deep in thought, and for the first time since his imprisonment the more unpleasant aspects of the episode faded into the background. He had other, far more interesting possibilities to consider.

CHAPTER FOUR

PETER KERSWELL settled back in his arm-chair deep in thought, oblivious to the muted rumble of London traffic in nearby St. James's Street. He wished Richard would soon return from visiting his tailor, there was a deal he wished to discuss with his friend. They had been settled in their Town apartments for less than a week, yet already the pasteboard invitations clustered thick upon the mantelshelf, but before they indulged themselves in the social whirl of the London Season there was the matter of Miranda's marriage to be considered.

For two years past the friends had shared a mutual London establishment. At first Peter had had elegantly furnished rooms of his own overlooking Piccadilly, but he had found the arrangement rather lonely. Used as he was to a large and gregarious family he found solitary living very depressing. True, upon occasion he had found some delightful female companion with whom to spend his bachelor hours, but these had been invariably short-term arrangements. When he could no longer stand eating alone, with only a servant or two hovering in attendance, he had suggested to Richard that they threw in their luck together. Richard had been only too delighted to agree, for he was even less well-equipped for solitary bachelorhood than Peter. His servants tended to grow unruly and his cook was seldom sober. At least under the rule of Mr. Kerswell the domestic arrangements were controlled and the meals edible.

Long before Richard returned home Miranda herself was announced, and Peter's face lit up.

"How provident. I was just thinking of you," he said.

"You were? Oh dear!"

"Why do you say 'oh dear' in such a way?"

"Because your thoughts so often lead to mischief."

Peter smiled wryly. "I suppose I deserve that. You know, since that rumpus at the boat-house I have never had a chance to speak to you alone to apologize properly. You were magnificent. I cannot think of anyone else who would have taken the whole fiasco so calmly."

"I assure you I would not have continued so calm if you had succeeded in marrying me off to your Cousin Denley," replied Miranda, her eyes twinkling. "I am only too happy to forget the whole incident provided that I have your promise that I can give my own approval before you embark upon any more of your escapades on my behalf."

"I promise," Peter smiled. "As I am sure Richard would, too, if he were here."

"Yes, where is my beloved brother?"

"At his tailor."

"Ah, a very serious errand. I fancy I shall have to leave before he returns. I only came to extend an invitation from Papa and myself to dine with us at Cavendish Square tomorrow."

"That would be delightful. I do not think that we are engaged. But do not run off yet. I have some books for you." He took two volumes from a small table. "There! *Ivanhoe*, a splendid tale by Sir Walter Scott. I enjoyed it enormously, and I am sure it will be to your taste. The other is one I know you have long sought. It is a little dog-eared, I am afraid, but the text is unimpaired. Rousseau's *Contrat Social*."

"How wonderful! I have heard much about *Ivanhoe*, and as for the Rousseau, you know that I have been searching for a copy these hundred years. You have read it?"

"Of course, and it contained many ideas I am sure you will find fascinating, only I beg of you keep it out of sight of Sir Henry. I fear the notion of a state run by the people as a whole might be too strong meat for him, and he will forbid me the house for feeding you such revolutionary theories."

"I will keep it hidden never fear," Miranda smiled. "What would I do without you to find the most interesting books for me?"

The fact that he possessed a keen inquiring mind was something Peter Kerswell preferred to keep hidden from most of the world. He chose to present a careless, light-hearted face to Society in general and many people, particularly his father, would have been surprised to learn just how wide and deep were his interests. Miranda was one of the few who knew of this side of his nature, for frequently he had smuggled books and pamphlets to her past the watchful guard of her conservative parent and brother.

"You would go out and find such inflammatory literature for yourself, which would disturb poor Sir Henry even more," Peter grinned. "So I beg you, be content to let me be your supplier."

"I shall be only too happy. But when I entered you said that you had been thinking about me. Am I permitted to know the course of your thoughts?"

"Yes. The subject was your impending marriage."

"Oh, so it is a certainty, is it?"

"Naturally. It is only the identity of the bridegroom that is in doubt. Now tell me, what steps have been taken in past years to introduce you to marriageable males?"

"The customary ones," replied Miranda, not at all put out by this rather unusual conversation. "I was trailed along to routs, soirées, and balls by my unfortunate Aunt Mountway. I hope you are not going to suggest that I go round the same course again. I had hoped that I had forsaken it for ever, particularly the balls. Dancing was never my forte, even if I ever found a partner tall enough to stand up with me."

"Yet you stand up with me very creditably."

"Only for the country dances at home, and you have height enough to look me in the eye. No, these fashionable balls fill me with terror, and I trip over my own feet, as well as everyone else's."

"Maybe you need some extra tuition. Perhaps a good dancing master—"

"Do you not recall how Papa used to engage them by the score, good, bad, and indifferent? They seldom lasted long, though I remember Monsieur de la Haye as the most spectacular. He was so distressed by my lack of ability that he locked himself in the servants' privy and wept, to everyone's great inconvenience."

"Yes, I do remember." Peter's face brightened at the recollection. "He would not come out, would he? Not until a live rat was introduced under the door."

"There is no need to guess whose idea that was."

Peter chuckled. "One of my more inspired suggestions, I think, as well as a particularly talented rat. I was deuced fond of him. I tamed him myself."

"Well, unless you have a further supply of tame rats, I suggest we abandon any thought of more dancing lessons."

"Perhaps you are right. Instead, I shall make another suggestion. Have you considered wearing a style of dress quite different from your normal? Something a little more colourful?"

Miranda looked down at her snuff-coloured muslin, part of a wardrobe of excellent quality but muted in tone, which had accumulated in her closet from comfort and expediency sooner than deliberate choice.

"What had you in mind?" she asked cautiously. "Though I must warn you that Madame Isabelle has already hinted most strongly that, while she is grateful for my custom, she would be just as grateful if I did not spread abroad the fact that she is my dressmaker."

"I just thought that a new approach to your dress might be a good idea, brighter hues, more spectacular colours. Look here, I borrowed this book of ladies' fashions from a friend. Give me your opinion. Would you not look splendid in one of these creations, in some striking colour—orange, maybe or a vivid green?"

He opened the publication at a page, and Miranda obediently took a look. The gowns illustrated were low cut and clinging, designed to show off attributes that Miranda certainly did not possess. The image of herself in any of them was too much. She collapsed into laughter.

"I will wager your friend does not live a hundred miles from Covent Garden," she chortled.

"Miranda!" Peter looked quite shocked. "You do not like them?"

Miranda wiped her eyes.

"I do think that they are exceedingly pretty. It is just that they may be a little unsuitable for me. It is a pity, for you have obviously gone to a deal of trouble on my behalf, but do not forget that I must be escorted by either Papa or Richard. Quite frankly, can you see either of them accompanying me anywhere in that gown at the top of the page, the one with the draped overskirt and very low *décolletage*? Particularly if it were in bright orange.''

''Not whilst absolutely sober,'' agreed Peter cheerfully. ''So that is another idea I shall discard. Perhaps we should try a change of social scene, since you are not happy with the usual assemblies and balls. Horses for courses, I always say.''

''Oh no! Not marriage to one of your Newmarket friends!'' protested Miranda. ''A horse is a worthy animal for transporting me from one place to another, and I am quite prepared to pat it, or feed it sugar, but the finer details of racing form are beyond me.''

''I did not mean it that way, you goose. Ah, here is Richard at long last. We can have his opinion now.''

''A glass of wine, I beg of you, before I expire from exhaustion!'' Richard burst into the room, immaculate from top to toe, looking anything but weary. He continued, ''That wretched tailor took an age with his pinning and his chalking, and I am still not convinced. Oh, hullo, Miranda. I did not expect to see you here.''

''I am here as a messenger, to invite you both to dine with us tomorrow, if you are free. Do you not admire Peter's latest plan to marry me off? He has a horse-coper marked out for my husband.''

''What?''

''Do not look so alarmed. Miranda is taking delight in misunderstanding me. My suggestion was that we should try some other section of society to find her a suitable spouse."

"A splendid idea!" Richard was full of enthusiasm which abruptly melted into bewilderment. "But what other section?"

"The political sphere, for example. We do not move much in such circles, do we? Yet Miranda would make an admirable politician's wife."

"Sounds a bit boring to me," said Richard, looking a little dismayed. "I mean, whatever would Papa and I talk to the fellow about when they come to dine at Branscombe Hall?"

"Or there is the Church. Do you know any bishops or deacons who need a wife?" asked Peter, seeing that his original suggestion had fallen upon stony ground.

"Not offhand," replied Richard. "That would seem to be the chief flaw in your scheme. How do we get to know people outside our own circle?"

"It would not seem to be too difficult," observed Miranda. "Judging by the number of invitations you have between you your own circle would seem to be pretty wide."

"An admirable idea!" Peter leapt to his feet and picked up the pile of gilt-edged invitation cards. "Let us go through these and see what we have. Mrs Brown-Smithers—no, we will know everyone there, and at the Rosswells', the Donningtons' and the Brands'. A dinner at General and Mrs. Hope's—their parties tend to be antediluvian, not a guest under eighty. A literary *soirée*—ah, that seems promising. 'Mrs. Amelia

Wordsworth-Pugh requests the pleasure' etc. Yes, this could be exactly what we are looking for."

"Who is Mrs. Wordsworth-Pugh?" demanded Miranda. "And how do you know her?"

"I cannot quite recollect at which function we were introduced, but I have a sharp memory of a prodigious set of puce plumes adorning the lady's head. She is the relict of Mr. Pugh, of Pugh's Patent Corsets. You must have heard of them, they are advertised most discreetly in all the best publications. She is a lady of large fortune and even larger ambition to make her mark in the world. Her *soirées* are quite the thing. We shall certainly go. I hear she has two uncommonly pretty daughters, too," Peter added as an afterthought.

"But we cannot all crowd in on your invitation," objected Richard, who found the prospect of both Mrs. Wordsworth-Pugh and literary society daunting.

"Yes, we can. It says 'Mr. Peter Kerswell and friends'. Cheer up, think of it as one more sacrifice for the benefit of Miranda," said Peter cheerfully.

"Or better still, think of the two pretty daughters," suggested Miranda with a smile.

"Ah, yes. Perhaps the evening will not be too disagreeable after all." Richard felt more comfortable.

"I think it promises to be quite amusing," said Miranda. "Provided, of course, that I am not obliged to wear a *décolletage* of bright orange."

"A *décolletage* of bright orange? I should hope not!" cried Richard in horror.

Peter only grinned and gave Miranda a huge wink as she departed.

At Mrs. Amelia Wordsworth-Pugh's elegantly appointed house in Great Brook Street all was in readiness for her *soirée*. Blazing flambeaux flanked the door, and ranks of powdered footmen lined the hall. The late Mr. Pugh had had the intelligence to invent a special corset, cleverly hinged to enable the wearer to sit in comfort, and because of this invention and his own tendency to overwork he had been able to leave his wife and daughters more than adequately provided for.

Mrs. Wordsworth-Pugh was ambitious for herself, and even more so for her daughters, but she had sense enough to realize that a fortune founded upon corsets, however ingenious, was not a suitable *entrée* into High Society. Therefore the lady sensibly cast round for some area in which she could establish herself with the maximum opportunity to shine without the risk of too many rebuffs. The realm of *les beaux arts* was ideal. She took care to invite a goodly sprinkling of prominent writers, artists, and musicians to her functions, and as the food was always good and the wine plentiful these affairs were invariably well attended.

Judging by the crush of carriages in Great Brook Street it appeared as if the world and his wife were beating a path to the Wordsworth-Pugh door. Miranda and her two escorts finally achieved the desired portals and were welcomed by their hostess, her extravagant plumes swaying alarmingly a good two feet above her head. Richard quelled a wince, for the plumes were puce and at sad variance with the brilliant yellow of the lady's gown.

Mrs. Wordsworth-Pugh saw nothing of his suppressed anguish, her sharp, calculating gaze was too busy assessing the newcomers. Miranda, being markedly plainer than either of her daughters, she greeted politely and immediately forgot. The two gentlemen were a different matter entirely. She looked them over, registered to the last guinea what would be the prospects of each, decided upon their eligibility, and greeted them most effusively as two more contenders for the hands of her Bella and her Lucy.

Peter, who knew very well his own value on the marriage market, guessed the reason for the lady's calculating look and permitted himself a secret chuckle. Richard could only be aware of those disastrous puce plumes, and was relieved to make his escape.

"There is quite a crush, to be sure," observed Peter, as they struggled through the throng in the elegant *salon*.

"How do we start looking for someone suitable for Miranda?"

"Do not make it too obvious, I beg of you," pleaded his sister. She was not absolutely sure she was doing the wisest thing by co-operating with the crazy plans of the pair of them. But, she observed to herself, it is better to know exactly what they are up to sooner than let it all come as a dreadful surprise.

"No indeed," said Peter. "Be casual about the whole thing. Mingle with the other guests, beg an introduction here, make a new acquaintance there, then at supper-time we will compare notes. But, by jove, if you will excuse me I will do a little mingling on my own account first. There is the most delectable little creature I have ever seen over there. No, by Harry, there are two of them! Can they be the Misses Wordsworth-Pugh, I wonder?"

"Why do you not both go over and find out?" suggested Miranda. "I have just seen someone whom I am certain is a friend of Hester Parkinson, so I must have a word with her."

"You do not mind?" Both men looked at her appealingly.

"Of course not. Hurry before those two beauties are snapped up by someone else not half so worthy."

She watched them go with considerable relief. While they were flirting on their own behalf they could do little damage on hers. She had not the slightest doubt that the ladies concerned would find them irresistible, for they were easily the two best-looking men there. Richard, handsome as ever, was superbly elegant in a coat of the finest blue wool, ornamented with flat gold buttons. Peter, too, who could look supremely well turned out when he bothered, had obviously deigned to stand still long enough for his valet to ensure that his green broadcloth frock-coat was immaculate, his neckwear *à l'orientale* a masterpiece of snowy muslin, and that his straw-coloured hair was brushed into sleek submission. Yes, Miranda was convinced that the two Misses Wordsworth-Pugh would need hearts of solid granite not to fall immediately in love with the pair of them. With a fond smile she went in search of her friend's friend.

The first part of the evening was devoted to things literary. A middle-aged gentleman, the editor of a fashionable satirical news-sheet, read a sharp, witty essay upon the perils of travel, a popular actress gave recitations from Shakespeare, and then a young poet read some of his own work. It was this last item which delighted Miranda the most. She was a voracious, if critical, reader of poetry, and she found the young man's verse both moving and original. Nor was she alone in her opinion. When the poet finished there was a moment's rapt silence before the applause broke out.

When supper was announced Miranda looked round to find Peter and Richard. It was no hard task. All she had to do was to find Miss Bella and Miss Lucy Wordsworth-Pugh; the young ladies were wearing pink and white plumes respectively, thankfully more restrained and more tasteful than their Mama's, and there were the two men.

"Hullo, Miranda. Are you enjoying yourself?" asked Richard, his eyes never for a second leaving the dimpled charms of Miss Lucy.

"Enormously, thank you," replied Miranda with perfect honesty. "I have met such a number of very interesting people."

"Anyone of particular significance?" asked Peter. He, too, was enraptured by his fair companion, Miss Bella, but he had not entirely forgotten the original purpose of their visit.

"One," replied Miranda, her eyes twinkling. "A most charming gentleman, a sculptor. There he is." She pointed out a small man, rotund of figure, his head totally devoid of hair.

Peter choked slightly at the sight, but Richard was so lost in the depths of Miss Lucy's pansy-blue eyes that all he said was, "Splendid. I am so glad you are finding the evening diverting."

"I can see that you are an original, Miss Branscombe," said Miss Bella, who was darker and more vivacious than her sister. "What did you think of Mr. Lehmann? Is not his poetry divine? And his looks so lean and torn by sensibility."

Miranda looked towards the young poet who was talking to a band of admirers. She noted his shabby coat and down-at-heel shoes as well as the poet's pale face and shadowed eyes. In her opinion hunger probably had more to do with his haunted romantic looks than poetic sensibility. She hoped that Mrs. Wordsworth-Pugh would feed him well.

Aloud she said, "I think he is the most promising poet I have come across in a long time. Although his work is full of originality there is something about it that is reminiscent of the early works of Lord Oxenham, do you not agree?"

"Most certainly. And do you not simply dote upon Lord Oxenham, for all people claim that he is so wicked? Mama pretends to be shocked by his behaviour, but I know for a fact that she always sends him an invitation to her *soirées*. He never comes, though." Miss Bella made an enchanting moue to show her disappointment.

The young lady was not to know it but for once her mother's persistence had paid dividends. Supper was almost over and the guests had drifted into little conversational groups when a new arrival was announced. Lord Oxenham! The stunned silence which fell upon the room was broken only by the sigh of rapture which burst unbidden from a score of female bosoms. He stood for a moment framed in the doorway so that the occupants of the room could get the full effect of his tall slender figure, clad as ever in dramatic black velvet.

As his hostess fairly sprinted forward to greet him Oxenham's dark brooding eyes ranged about the room looking for some hope of dissipating the ennui which was his constant companion. An ancient title had been his at fifteen, along with a vast fortune. At eighteen literary acclaim had been heaped upon him for his poetry, which, along with a pale handsome face, a superb profile, and a taste for the dramatic in his personal life, had made him the darling of London Society. Every fashionable lady, young and not so young, who was worth her salt was madly in love with Lord Oxenham. Everything the world had to offer was his by the time his lordship had reached one-and-twenty, so that he had spent the ensuing decade trying to find ways of passing the rest of his mortal span without being bored. This desperate searching had resulted in some dark whispers about his morals and his honour. He had been dubbed the Wicked Lord, a title which had, of course, made him all the more sought after in fashionable circles.

When all else failed, Oxenham attempted to while away the tedious hours by arriving unexpectedly at some minor function. The stir that this created was almost gratifying, and it gave him a fleeting amusement to raise his hostess's social credit by his mere presence, only to deflate it again by cutting her dead for the rest of the Season.

Lord Oxenham groaned inwardly, ignoring Mrs. Wordsworth-Pugh's gabbled welcome and her agitated plumes which wagged perilously close to his face. He had been a fool to come. It was the same dreary old scene, a pseudo-literary *soirée*, crammed with minor talents and inferior intellects. The dark eyes searched the sea of faces, all so eager and so abysmally adoring. If only they could rest upon something or someone that promised diversion. The only novelty was an exceedingly tall young lady at the back of the room who was deep in conversation with a small bald man. The fact that she was paying no heed to Oxenham was unusual, but more than that, she was extremely plain.

The plainest female that his lordship had ever seen, in fact. He had paid attention to plenty of beautiful women, for they threw themselves at his feet in droves, but he had never before singled out a plain one. That, at least, should set the company by the heels. Yes, it might prove nearly amusing, and besides, it was the best that the evening had to offer.

"I wish to be introduced to the young lady in the tabby gown," Oxenham said imperiously, blocking poor Mrs. Wordsworth-Pugh halfway through her eulogy on his latest book of poems.

"Why—why, of course, my lord," stammered the unfortunate hostess, overcome by sudden panic at not being able to remember the name of this fortunate young lady.

"Miss Miranda Branscombe, Mama," Miss Bella hissed in her ear.

"Why yes, to be sure. Miss Branscombe, may I have the pleasure of presenting to you Lord Oxenham?"

Miranda looked up in surprise to find herself the object of attention of the whole room, her companion of a moment ago, the little sculptor, having been swept aside by the throng like a small green beetle. In his place stood a tall, handsome gentleman with a decidedly disdainful expression on his face.

Oxenham waited for the usual rapture. This young lady would blush, stammer, be utterly confused, then rattle on for a space about how excessively she loved his works. He was quite accustomed to this reaction and had learnt to wait until it had subsided before any normal conversation could commence. He was about to suffer a shock, for no blush stained Miranda's cheek; she was quite incapable of gushing, and she was perfectly lucid and understandable from her very first word.

"My lord, I am truly pleased to meet you," she said, smiling calmly and extending her hand. "I have long wished to make your acquaintance, for there is something I am eager to know and only you can supply the answer. What sort of rig do you intend for your new yacht?"

Lord Oxenham, executing the normal civilities, froze in mid-bow.

"I beg your pardon?" he asked in astonishment.

"Your new yacht, the one you are having built in Bray's Yard, how do you propose to have her rigged? The yard is not above two miles from my home and some of our people work there. Your craft has excited great interest, may I say, as well as gratitude, for things have been rather slack since the end of the war. Do you intend to sail her far?"

Used to choosing his own subjects for conversation, Lord Oxenham suffered some difficulty in adjusting his thoughts.

"Er—yes—to the Mediterranean. Perhaps further," he managed to utter.

"Then you were wise to insist upon such width in the beam. Mr. Bray was a little concerned that she would not be excessively speedy, but clearly you prefer cruising to racing. He will be relieved. The seaworthiness will naturally be a foregone conclusion. Mr. Bray is a master of his craft.''

"He came to see me well recommended, and I was particularly pleased with the designs he produced.'' Now that he had grown used to this topic, so unexpected at a London *soirée*, Oxenham was quite content to continue. If there was one thing that laid claim to his affections, other than himself, it was his love-affair with the sea.

"Now that is mock modesty, my lord, for Mr. Bray told me himself that a good three-quarters were your own work, he merely transferred your ideas into working drawings. He was extremely impressed by your schemes for using the deck space to advantage.''

Lord Oxenham had never before been accused of modesty. This was a new experience. His customary boredom made an attempt to assert itself, but was vanquished by an unexpected twinge of pleasure. Praise from a craftsman of Bray's measure was praise worth having. Oxenham seated himself next to Miranda.

"It took a deal of concentration, I can assure you,'' he said, settling himself comfortably. "I cut model after model of the deck plan from paper before I was satisfied.''

"What can Lord Oxenham be talking about to that Branscombe girl? They have had their heads together this age,'' demanded Mrs. Wordsworth-Pugh's sister-in-law, plain Miss Pugh.

"Yes, is it not delightful? His lordship suffers so terribly from ennui that he never stays anywhere above half an hour. Why, at Lady Bradbury's he was gone within ten minutes, yet he has been here over five-and-forty minutes already and shows no sign of leaving." The puce plumes, those barometers of Mrs. Wordsworth-Pugh's every mood, danced ecstatically at this unexpected social coup. The success of her little *salon* was assured for the rest of the Season at least.

"I do not know what he sees in her," continued Miss Pugh waspishly. "Horse-faced creature, if you ask me, and her fortune is nothing to shout about. Bella and Lucy are ten times as handsome and twice as well provided for, yet he has not looked in their direction at all. It is not fair!"

Mrs. Wordsworth-Pugh did not agree. She was a very fond mama, as well as an ambitious one, and her keen eyes had been on her girls all evening, so she could not help but notice that they had a new beau apiece. Mr. Branscombe and Mr. Kerswell were nice, unexceptional young gentlemen, well worth cultivating. Their prospects were promising—Mrs. Wordsworth-Pugh had taken care to confirm this fact within half an hour of them crossing her threshold—and though Mr. Branscombe was the more handsome and would inherit the more ancient title, Mr. Kerswell was very agreeable and would come into the larger fortune. A sharp vein of sense ran through Mrs. Wordsworth-Pugh's plans for her daughters. She was perfectly aware of Oxenham's dubious reputation, and whereas she was delighted to have him at her *soirée* she was quite happy to have him dangle after some other female sooner than one of her daughters. If Bella and Lucy could ensnare the likes of Mr. Branscombe and Mr. Kerswell she could be quite content. Those two young gentlemen might be less spectacular than his lordship but as sons-in-law they would be a deal more comfortable.

"Let dear Lord Oxenham prattle to whom he will," she declared. "So long as he remains in my *salon* my evening will be judged an unqualified success. That is all I care about."

Indeed his lordship showed no signs of moving. He and Miranda had been engaged in a long and detailed discussion on yachting and the sea in general and for once Oxenham was oblivious to time. It was Miranda who broke up the conversation.

"If you will excuse me, my Lord," she said, rising from her chair, "there is Mr. Spiro about to leave and I must have a word with him. He has just completed a statue of Apollo ready to cast it in bronze and he has invited me to see how it is done. I must get the directions of the foundry—all I know is that it is somewhere in Whitechapel."

Lord Oxenham was astounded. This young lady was preparing to leave him, and he had not yet indicated that he was weary of her company! Such a thing had not happened to him in years! He started to summon up his indignation, ready to treat this extraordinary

Miss Branscombe to one of his cool, haughty stares, but before he had half begun curiosity overtook him.

"A foundry? You would go to a foundry?"

"Certainly. I have never been to one before, have you? It should be most interesting, and, I dare say, exciting, with the furnace and the molten metal. Mr. Spiro warned me it would be rather dirty so I shall dress accordingly. You do not mind if I leave you now? You will not be lonely? Besides, you have set convention by the ears enough for one evening."

"What do you mean?"

Miranda's eyes sparkled with mirth.

"Why, by conversing all evening with the plainest female here. It is sure to be a talking-point, you know."

This observation was so close to his original motives that Lord Oxenham almost found himself spluttering a denial, but he was saved from this indignity by Miranda insisting that she should take her leave of him. He watched her tall, dowdily clad figure cross the room, his thoughts in something of a turmoil. It had been the most peculiar evening, not at all what he had intended. Why, he had talked to one female for well over an hour without touching upon his favourite subject—himself. Moreover, that hour had gone more swiftly than any he could remember in a long time. Miranda Branscombe gave him the odd feeling that she could read his thoughts, for she had known at once his reasons for engaging her in conversation, but stranger still, as she had left him she had asked most kindly if he would be lonely. No one had ever recognized the deep loneliness of the much fêted, publicly adored Lord Oxenham before. That knowledge left him feeling shaken.

Suddenly he looked about the room. Everyone was regarding him expectantly, wondering where his favours would rest next. He glared at the circle of faces and found them appallingly insipid so that he could not bear to remain. He strode quickly to the door, bidding his hostess an abrupt farewell. On his way he passed Miranda who was deep in conversation with her diminutive sculptor.

"Miss Branscombe, I wish you good night," Oxenham said curtly. "And if your friend cares to send me an invitation to the casting of his statue you may tell him that I shall attend."

With that he swept out, leaving an excited buzz of conversation in his wake.

Oxenham's departure belatedly reminded Richard and Peter that they had been sorely lax in their chaperoning of Miranda; they had both been rather too busy evading the chaperon of Miss Bella and Miss Lucy. Now they came forward to escort Miranda home, not certain whether to be pleased or sorry that she had got herself so noticed.

"Whatever did you talk about?" asked Richard, who could not comprehend holding a conversation with someone on Oxenham's intellectual plane.

"Boats," replied Miranda.

"Boats?" Richard's voice rose to a squeak. "Oh Miranda! Ladies do not converse about such a subject! What will his lordship think?"

"He seemed quite entertained," replied Miranda calmly.

Peter, as always less innocent in the ways of the world than his friend, had misgivings on another quarter.

"How did he behave towards you?" he demanded suspiciously. "No luring you into private rooms or secluded corners, I hope? If so I shall be round to see him instanter!"

"Steady on, that is my duty! I am Miranda's brother!" declared Richard.

"But I am more Oxenham's weight," stated Peter in a no-nonsense voice.

Miranda burst out laughing at the pair of them.

"There is no need to get agitated, my virtue was quite safe. His lordship behaved with the utmost propriety and we were within sight of upwards of twenty people the whole time, which is more than can be said for Miss Bella or Miss Lucy."

"They were perfectly safe, they were in the conservatory with us," said Richard, with such innocence that Miranda burst out laughing again.

"Well, we need not concern ourselves about Lord Oxenham, then," said Peter hurriedly, "for I doubt if we will meet him again."

"I will," said Miranda, her eyes wide and guileless.

"What! Where?" Both young men sat bolt upright from the carriage squabs. They had missed Oxenham's parting remarks as he had left the *soirée*.

"At Whitechapel."

"Whitechapel? What on earth will you be doing there? No one, absolutely no one, goes to Whitechapel except by accident!" cried Richard in horror.

"I am going to watch the casting of a bronze statue."

"But that will be most disagreeable, all dirt and soot! No, the whole thing is impossible. You cannot go alone, and I am sorry, Miranda, I would make many sacrifices for your sake, but spending a day in a Whitechapel foundry is not one of them!" Richard's tone was unusually final.

Peter, however, had seen the determined look in Miranda's eye.

"Richard is right, you cannot go alone," he said. "So I will come with you, if you wish, though why you should think Oxenham will visit such a place is more than I can fathom."

"He said he would come, in front of half the guests at Mrs. Wordsworth-Pugh's."

"He did? In that case wild horses would not keep me away. Not for a fortune would I miss seeing Whitechapel turned into a fashionable venue for Society. You should come too, Richard. It looks as if everyone will be there."

"You think so? Even Miss Lucy?" Richard brightened.

"Certainly Miss Lucy and Miss Bella if their Mama has any say in the matter," said Miranda.

"We will both definitely come," replied Peter and Richard in unison.

"It has been a most remarkable evening," said Peter as he and Richard entered their bachelor apartments after having deposited Miranda at Cavendish Square. "I did not think Oxenham seemed anything remarkable close to, did you?"

"I scarcely noticed him," confessed Richard. "All I saw was Miss Lucy. Is she not the most adorable creature you ever saw?"

"Very pretty indeed, though my taste was more for the livelier character of Miss Bella. Now do not look at me so! You do not want us to be rivals for the same lady, do you? Yes, I think we were wise to widen our horizons. It was not a deal of help to Miranda, for she spent most her time chatting to Oxenham instead of looking for a possible husband, but she seemed happy enough, and for my part I found it very enjoyable. What is that you have in your hand?"

Richard held out a small piece of pasteboard.

"We have a visitor in our absence seemingly," he said.

Peter looked at the expensively engraved name and let out a shout of laughter.

"Cousin Denley, by all that's wonderful! And here in London! Usually he hates the place! Perhaps our search for a husband for Miranda may be nearing its end after all."

CHAPTER FIVE

"JUST THE MEREST SLIVER of broiled capon, if you please, Miss Branscombe. Anything more would be quite beyond my digestion," Arnold Denley declared, as Miranda pressed him to sample some of the numerous delicacies with which the table was laden.

"Are you sure? The haddock is plainly baked and wholesome if you have it without the sauce, and the fricassee of veal is not over rich, I promise you." Miranda looked doubtfully at the meagre slice of poultry isolated on the expanse of dinner-plate.

"No, no, I thank you! The capon will more than suffice. I am sure I shall not sleep tonight as it is. I live so quietly at home that the excitement of dining out will agitate my nerves, I know it will."

Miranda's eyes sparkled. Mr. Denley would have to work hard to inflame even his nerves because of so modest a table. The dinner-party at Cavendish Square was little more than a family affair, and Peter and Richard could be entirely discounted from the conversation, for they were both completely taken up with the two Wordsworth-Pugh girls.

"I should be sorry if our evening caused you any discomfort," she said gravely. "But if it does, I have heard that warm milk and seltzer is a good remedy for the combined ills of dyspepsia and sleeplessness.''

''Is it really? Now that is something new, I shall try it this evening without fail.'' Mr. Denley laid aside his knife and fork for a moment and wrote down this discovery in a small notebook with great deliberation, then he beamed at Miranda. Knowledge of a new medicine was enough to set the seal on his happiness at any time, and the fact that Miss Branscombe had been the one to provide this latest addition in his formidable collection was most satisfying. It strengthened his growing belief that here might be the ideal wife for someone with so frail and delicate a constitution as his own.

''It is very kind of you and Sir Henry to invite me to dine,'' he said. ''And me not in Town above eight-and-forty hours. Naturally, on my first day I did not stir from my bed—that would have been crass folly. I needed a good rest to recover from the rigours of the journey else I dared not answer for the consequences. What it is to be a martyr to one's health! I find the travelling so arduous that I have not been to London these five years, and indeed, if I did not have a very strong incentive this time I would have stayed away for the rest of the brief span left to me upon this earth.''

''May one ask the nature of this incentive?'' asked Miranda, who was beginning to harbour suspicious thoughts.

''Why, Harley Street, madam!'' replied Mr. Denley in some astonishment. ''Why else would I come but to consult the finest medical authorities in the land? I would risk the perils of the long journey for nothing less. I have come to see if one of the eminent doctors can find a cure for my condition, even though I know it is hopeless. Still, I feel I owe it to myself and to my dear friends to struggle bravely to the bitter end, trying all avenues left open to me." His thoughts might be toying with matrimony, but while there remained those fascinating members of the medical profession to be consulted Mr. Denley would leave the benefits of wedlock to wait their turn.

"Oh!" Miranda uttered an exclamation that was suspiciously like a sigh of relief. Silently she offered an apology to Peter and Richard, for she had been nursing the dread suspicion that it was their fault that Mr. Denley had arrived so unexpectedly upon the scene. Apparently the initiative had been all Mr. Denley's own.

It was then that Peter temporarily prized his attention away from Miss Bella's delightful chatter, and Miranda caught his gaze across the table as it shifted from her to his frail cousin. There was a speculative glint in those green eyes that made her heart sink, and she determined to nip any prospective schemes in the bud as soon as possible.

"Before you make any further plans the answer is a firm and definite no," she said to him later, as she poured his coffee in the withdrawing-room.

"I think we are in no doubt as to the answer. Now all that bothers me is the question," he replied, helping himself to sugar.

"The question is would I care to marry your Cousin Denley?"

"I thought that business was all settled among the bullrushes at New Park."

"So did I, but I had not counted on Mr. Denley reappearing in my life like a latter-day Moses."

Peter gave a snort of laughter.

"I am sure the Biblical Moses was a deal more amusing. Look at my cousin now deep in monologue with Miss Bella. One can scarcely call it conversation for the poor girl has not managed to open her mouth once. You must admit, though, that since he is in Town anyway, and as we still have not found you a prospective husband—"

"There you have it to perfection. I still have not found a prospective husband. I fear Mr. Denley will have to be wasted."

"Ah well!" Peter gave a mock sigh. "Our loss will be Harley Street's gain no doubt. If you will excuse me I will go and rescue Miss Bell."

"I think you should," agreed Miranda. "The poor girl is looking a little pale. I fear your cousin's diatribes do require a strong stomach at times."

"One a deal stronger than mine, especially during meals," agreed Peter, and he strolled in the direction of the delectable Miss Bella.

Bereft of his latest audience Mr. Denley attached himself to his hostess with such renewed vigour that Miranda was forced to keep her eyes averted from Peter's teasing gaze. Richard noticed nothing of her predicament, his horizons were happily and completely encompassed by Miss Lucy.

Sir Henry Branscombe had greeted the unexpected arrival of Mr. Denley with hopefulness. True, he had been assured by his son a couple of weeks since that all chance of an alliance was at an end; but he was not so certain. These young fellows thought they knew everything, but in affairs of the heart there was no knowing how things might turn out. He could only wish that the gentleman in question had a more cheerful turn of conversation. Still, it looked as though the problem of Miranda might be solved. Poor Sir Henry, as one difficulty seemed vanquished so another loomed immediately upon the horizon in the shape of Mrs. Wordsworth-Pugh.

Once her daughters were nicely settled perhaps she could give a little thought to her own future, a wealthy, well-preserved widow on the right side of forty (if one was not too nice about the truth). Mrs. Wordsworth-Pugh looked in the direction of Sir Henry Branscombe, her plumes fairly bristling with romantic intentions.

Sir Henry caught her expression and recognized it at once. As a widower of more than twenty years' standing he was quite accustomed to being the object of matrimonial desires, and equally accustomed to taking avoiding action, for he was quite happy with his present state and had no wish to alter it. However, some instinct recognized in Mrs. Wordsworth-Pugh a more than ordinary adversary. Moreover, there were those plumes to contend with. Why the lady had chosen that particular puce colour to go with a gown that was of definite shrimpish hue was more than he could understand. The incredible fact that perhaps Mrs. Wordsworth-Pugh actually liked the combination of colours was too horrible to contemplate. Sir Henry backed away from the lady and her intentions as much as his duties as host would allow—to no avail. Mrs. Wordsworth-Pugh had been repulsed before but had never allowed it to spoil her campaign. Her sights were set very firmly upon Sir Henry, and the poor man trembled in his elegant kid slippers.

"You are going to the Whitechapel Foundry on Tuesday, are you not, Sir Henry?" cooed Mrs. Wordsworth-Pugh winsomely. "It will be the most unusual event of the Season without a doubt. We would not miss it for the world."

"Alas—madam—a prior engagement—" Sir Henry began to stutter, then to his great relief his son came to his rescue.

"Whitechapel Foundry? Why, of course we will be there!" declared Richard positively, his eyes never leaving Lucy's face. A new opportunity to be with his beloved could not be rejected.

Richard had another reason for attending this most unlikely of society functions—to prevent his sister,

Miranda, from appearing too eccentric. However, as their carriage moved into Fenchurch Street on the appointed day he became extremely glad that he had come.

"There are some very well-turned-out rigs going our way," he remarked, as a stylish phaeton overtook them.

"Indeed there are. Is it my imagination or is half of fashionable London heading east?" asked Peter.

"I think you are right," agreed Miranda. "I have already recognized several people who were at the Wordsworth-Pugh *soirée*. I wonder if bronze-casting might be the coming thing, and that every man of fashion will soon have his own foundry and crucible as now he has his carriage and his box at the theatre?"

"Oh, I hope not. It is an occupation I am sure I am most unfitted for. Oh, you are funning, are you not?" Richard smiled at his own foolishness and went back to watching through the carriage window for some sign of the Wordsworth-Pugh coach.

"Most of these people are simply going to gawp at Lord Oxenham," said Miranda. "I am convinced that many of them would attend the slaughter-house if they thought he would be there. Poor man, it must be very trying to be so stared at."

"You do not think he courts such attention?" asked Peter.

"I am not sure. Perhaps he has had it thrust upon him for so long that now he cannot abandon the habit.

Fame came to him so uncomfortably young, it must have been a terrible drawback. I do feel sorry for him."

Peter gave a chuckle. "I warrant you must be the only female in London who pities Oxenham. All the rest would eat him for dinner if they could."

"Perhaps you are right." Miranda gave a smile. "Anyway, I fear that many of these people are on a wild-goose chase for I doubt if Lord Oxenham will come. I hear he is rather capricious in his plans."

"That is true. Hullo, we have stopped." Peter put his head out of the carriage window to address his coachman. "What is amiss, Jenkins?"

"The road ahead is jammed proper with traffic, sir," Jenkins informed him. "If I go on there will be no way of extricating us. I fear you will have to walk the rest of the way."

"Goodness, he is right!" said Richard, putting down the other window. "Did you ever see such a crush?"

"I warrant the people of Whitechapel have not," observed Miranda. "Look, they are lining the streets as though this were a royal procession."

True enough, the hard-working residents of Whitechapel had never before experienced such an influx of splendidly dressed folk on their streets, and they were determined to make the most of this spectacle. They crowded the thoroughfares and hung from every window, observing the elegant carriages and commenting loudly and critically upon the fashionable dress.

"We will never manage it through this crush!" declared Richard.

"There must be a way. I am sure these two stout fellows could get us through for a crown a piece," said Peter, indicating two hefty workmen who were audibly discussing the high-quality craftsmanship of his carriage.

"For a crown a piece we'd lift yer up and fly yer there, guv'nor." beamed one of the men.

"We will be tolerably content to stay on our own two feet if you will but conduct us to Fox's Metal Manufactory," said Peter.

"Easy as winkin'. Follow us, if yer please. Hey, make way there. Mind yer backs!"

With a combination of brute strength and local knowledge their guides led them through a maze of back alleys before finally leaving them at the gates of the foundry off Montague Street. The squat stone-walled building was already hot enough from the furnace, but the discomfort was increased by the number of people who had squeezed themselves into the building, the yard, and even the road outside.

"Well, this may be the strangest event of the Season, but I fancy all we will see will be the head of the person in front," said Miranda.

"Be content that we are here. Think of all the unfortunate wretches who are sitting comfortably in their clubs at this moment or strolling beneath the trees in the park. How envious they must be to be missing this.

To expect to actually see anything is to be unreasonable,'' Peter admonished her with mock severity.

"I am torn to bits," protested Richard. "This coat will never be fit to wear again it has been so pulled about, and look, I am covered in dirt." He brushed away a minute speck of soot that marred his snowy shirt-front.

"Do not worry, it gives you a decidedly raffish air," comforted Miranda. "Oh, there is Mr. Spiro! How hot and bothered he looks. See, he is waving to us."

Indeed, the little sculptor, perspiring freely, had managed to scramble precariously on to some sort of ledge and was surveying the crowd. Catching sight of Miranda's tall figure he waved vigorously and called, "Miss Branscombe, I have a place saved for you at the front. Make way for Miss Branscombe and her party, I beg of you ladies and gentleman. Make way!"

Richard groaned somewhere deep in the crush. For all the fashionable elements present he was still not convinced that this was the sort of occasion where Miranda ought to be conspicuous. However, he had no option but to follow her as they were gradually pushed to the front. Mr. Spiro greeted them effusively.

"Dear Miss Branscombe, who would have imagined such a success?" he beamed. "It is all due to you! Do you know, already I have sold my Apollo for two hundred guineas, and it is not even cast yet. How can I thank you?"

"No thanks are necessary. I did nothing at all."

"Nothing at all!" The little sculptor flung up his hands. "All you did was to show a real interest in my work, then to pass on that interest to your friend, Lord Oxenham, and where his lordship goes all London will follow. You may call it nothing, but I still declare that I am eternally in your debt."

Miranda was about to protest further that she could not claim Lord Oxenham as a friend when there was a stirring and a murmuring in the crowd, and the noble gentleman himself emerged. Such was his reputation and his bearing that there had been no pushing a way through for him, the people had fallen back of their own accord.

"Miss Branscombe, your servant!" He bowed to Miranda and coolly ignored everyone else.

"My lord, I am so glad you are here. Things are about to commence, are they not, Mr. Spiro? And it would have been such a shame for you to have missed anything so interesting."

Oxenham stared about him at the dirt, the soot-encrusted walls, the grubby floor littered with scrap metal, and wondered what on earth had possessed him to come. What could interest him in this hell-hole? However, since he had made the effort to attend they might as well get on with it.

"Begin!" he said imperiously, and glared at Mr. Spiro.

The poor sculptor stared back at this force in the fashionable world, opened his mouth and found that he could not utter a word. He had practised pretty

speeches, clever explanations of the processes, and
erudite comments upon artistic matters ever since he
had been so unexpectedly "taken up" by Society, but
now that he was confronted by the acknowledged
master of it all he had dried up completely.

"I think that the lion's share of the work has been
done already," said Miranda, stepping into the breach.
"You have been very busy."

She addressed her remarks to Mr. Fox, owner of the
establishment and master founder. This worthy fellow was not at all awed by the sudden interest excited
by his craft; it had fascinated him for the fifty-odd
years of his life so it only seemed reasonable that the
rest of the world would catch on to its attraction
eventually.

"That I have, miss," he replied. "Me and my boys.
Today's little bit of work'll only be a small part of the
happenings."

"What do you do first, light your furnace?" Miranda was enjoying her different surroundings and eager to learn all she could.

"Bless you, miss, no! There was a deal to do afore
we gets to firing up. There was the arranging for the
moulds to be made of Mr. Spiro's statue. We go to my
brother-in-law, Ned Harris, for those, and they must
be skillfully made, believe me, for no amount of our
skill will make up for a bad mould."

On went Mr. Fox, telling of the processes, the
smelting, the hazards to be avoided. He spoke clearly
and fluently, for he was used to explaining the work

carefully, having trained his four sons in a craft that was difficult and potentially dangerous. He addressed his remarks to the tall young lady who was so inordinately interested in everything, and if the haughty gent in the black velvet cared to listen too, then he did not mind. Mr. Fox was not nervous of Lord Oxenham as Mr. Spiro had been. Since Mr. Fox did not frequent White's or Boodles, and his lordship was not a *habitué* of the Loyal East London Friendly Society or the "Bird In Hand" the master founder was happily unaware of his visitor's formidable reputation.

Miranda's absorption in the proceedings was infectious, so that Lord Oxenham found himself keeping close so as not to miss a single word. Now and again he continued to wonder at himself for being there at all; but if his thoughts dwelt too long on those lines he found that he missed something that Fox was saying, and Fox was most unexpectedly interesting.

The actual pouring came at last, with gasps as the fiery metal was tipped gently into the mould and much cheering when the feat was accomplished. Then it was all over. The crowd that had struggled so hard to arrive struggled even harder to leave, pausing only to drop tokens of appreciation, in the shape of guineas and half-guineas, into a bucket placed at the door by a delighted Mr. Fox. Everyone was satisfied. They had participated in the same event as Lord Oxenham, been extremely uncomfortable and seen a sizeable slice of fashionable London suffer likewise. The event had been a success. Only Richard was not happy, for he had not been able to speak to Miss Lucy. The unmistakable plumes of her Mama could be seen waving distinctly not a dozen yards away, but a phalanx of tightly packed bodies had proved an impenetrable barrier. As Richard left to push his way to the Wordsworth-Pugh family through the lessening mass Mr. Spiro came puffing towards Miranda, his face perspiring more than ever.

"Miss Branscombe, my lord, gentlemen, what a triumph!" At last his voice had overcome its terror of Oxenham. "One hundred invitations to my forthcoming exhibition have been accepted! One hundred! What an idea that was of yours, Miss Branscombe."

Oxenham raised a sardonic eyebrow.

"Your idea, Miss Branscombe?" he asked.

"I merely suggested to Mr. Spiro that as it seemed likely that many influential people would attend today's little gathering many of them might show an even greater interest in his work if he were to stage an exhibition and to bring the invitations along."

"You intend setting up as a patroness of the arts and having your own *salon*, Miss Branscombe?" asked Oxenham.

Miranda laughed heartily at the idea.

"No, not at all. Mr. Spiro is a most worthy and talented person, and if I can ever help him by showing some attention or doing him a kindness then I am happy."

"Oh, a kindness!" said Oxenham as though it were some rare and seldom-used word. He was a little put out, for he was not used to ladies laughing at his words. Sighing, weeping, tearing out their hair on his account—yes! But laughing at him—definitely no!

"Miss Branscombe is always doing kindnesses for people!" declared Peter hotly, imagining that he detected some hint of criticism in Oxenham's words.

"Oh?" Oxenham gave a cold hard glare in Peter's direction, but since that young man declined to wilt under the onslaught it was a sadly wasted effort. The amusement of the day was over, and the boring prospect of the remaining empty hours depressed his lordship. Half a day left of utter tedium! How would he survive?

His gloomy thoughts were interrupted by the hurried reappearance of Richard.

"Miranda, can you come?" he asked urgently. "You will never guess who is out here! Mr. Denley! And I am afraid he has been taken ill."

Arnold Denley lay in the yard, stretched out on a cart like some ancient hero upon his funeral bier. His thoughts were far from heroic, however, for he felt exceedingly faint and unwell. To add to his misery he was being ministered to by Mrs. Wordsworth-Pugh, a most kind and well-meaning lady but one who did not understand the art of administering a smelling-bottle half so well as Miss Branscombe. How he wished that Miss Branscombe would come and make him feel comfortable again before his nose grew quite raw from the ammonia fumes. It was on her account that he had come to this dreadful place—though to be honest he had also fostered some notion of placing an order for a tasteful funerary vase, an elegant Grecian urn in bronze perhaps. The more he saw of Miranda Branscombe the more he was convinced that she would make him an ideal wife, and though he was painfully ignorant of the art of courtship he knew that pursuit came into it somewhere. Now he felt that he had been rash to the point of folly to have pursued Miss Branscombe to Whitechapel. He should have waited and given chase in some more convivial surroundings that would not have taxed his strength.

"Oh, poor Mr. Denley. How pale you look."

At the sound of Miranda's voice he opened his eyes a little.

"Miss Branscombe, I am dying," he groaned.

"He just toppled over like a ninepin," explained Mrs. Wordsworth-Pugh, thrusting the smelling-bottle a little closer to Mr. Denley's suffering nostrils.

"He is not going to die, is he?" cried Miss Lucy, her pretty face crumpled in horror.

"Of course not," Richard rushed to reassure her. "My sister will know what to do to help him recover in no time. Pray take my arm, we will move and let Miranda take charge." And he led his beloved firmly from the scene just in case Denley did prove ungallant enough to expire in her presence.

"I expect it was the heat," said Miranda, loosening Mr. Denley's cravat for him, and gently removing the smelling-salts from Mrs. Wordsworth-Pugh's enthusiastic grasp. "It is an excessively warm day, quite apart from the effects of the furnace."

"I could not get my breath. There was no air and such a crush. I was suffocating—suffocating." Mr. Denley recalled his ordeal with dramatic relish.

"There, there, put it out of your mind. It is all over now. You will soon recover." Miranda spoke with calm consideration. "I will soak my handkerchief in lavender water and put it on your brow, so—and if this cart could be moved across the yard. There, that is better is it not, Mr. Denley, now that you are in the shade?"

"Oh much, much better." With someone to minister to him so competently Mr. Denley was feeling almost happy.

"As soon as you feel up to it we will have your carriage brought round to the gate, and your coachman will have you home in no time, Cousin Denley," Peter assured him.

Alas, his kindness was misplaced. Mr. Denley's eyes flew open in panic.

"I could not bear to ride all that way, not on such a stifling day! It would kill me, I know it would! Air! I need air! What am I to do? Help me, dear Miss Branscombe! Help me!"

"You could lodge where you are until nightfall, and imbibe the full benefits of the atmosphere of Whitechapel," said Oxenham acidly. He was being ignored, a state of affairs totally repulsive to him.

"Lord Oxenham likes to joke, Mr. Denley," said Miranda quickly. Poor little man, he really was upset. She could not let him down. She continued, "Do not distress yourself, I will think of some way to get you home without a tedious journey, never fear."

Totally convinced, Arnold Denley gave a little sigh and closed his eyes again.

"Have you any notion how you are to arrange for transport, now that you have discarded carriages? I have heard that ballooning is an excellent means of travel. It would seem to be your only alternative," said Lord Oxenham, a mite sarcastically.

"Obviously your acquaintance with Miss Branscombe is slight, otherwise you would be well aware that her ingenuity knows no bounds. If she says she will find a way of getting my cousin home with the least amount of distress then that is exactly what she will do," said Peter with authority. Oxenham's manner irritated him excessively, forcing him to prove his own superiority. However, where Miranda was concerned he knew that he was on to a safe bet, for knowledge born of long custom told him that when she had such a firm glint in her eye she could accomplish anything.

"I do not intend to dispense with carriages entirely," said Miranda. "Mr. Denley, you could suffer a short coach-ride, could you not? A distance of about a mile?"

"I— I think so, if you consider it necessary, Miss Branscombe," answered Denley, summoning up his reserves of fortitude.

"But that leaves you near enough four miles short of home by my reckoning," commented Lord Oxenham.

"Which we will travel most pleasantly by river," said Miranda.

"By river?" Half a dozen pairs of eyes stared at her.

"Certainly. Why not? We are not so very far from the Thames here, and it would be much more cool and refreshing to travel thus, sooner than go by road on such a day."

"Not to mention less odorous. It is a capital scheme!" Peter gave it his immediate approval.

"Indeed it is! Perhaps the ladies would join us too?" Richard had returned to the group in time to hear this new proposal, and now his eyes gazed beseechingly at Lucy.

"Oh please, Mama, may we?" The two sisters turned to their mother.

Mrs. Wordsworth-Pugh had intercepted the look between Richard and her younger daughter, and immediately decided that such a splendid opportunity might cement the promising relationship a little further. True, a river-trip under such a broiling sun would certainly scorch her daughters' complexions abominably, but the sacrifice would be worthwhile. Besides, cucumbers were cheap at this time of year and would soon repair the damage.

"I think such an expedition sounds quite delightful," agreed Mrs. Wordsworth-Pugh, her plumes a-quiver.

"But what of Mr. Denley? What is his opinion? After all it is for his benefit," said Miranda, though she scarcely needed to enquire. Arnold Denley was looking at her with gratitude and utter devotion.

"Miss Branscombe, you are my saviour. To journey upon the water will be so refreshing it will restore me in no time, I am sure," he replied.

"There, that is all settled," said Peter with satisfaction, for now he could be in Miss Bella's company a little longer. "Once on the river Cousin Denley will soon be feeling chirpy again so this promises to be a merry little outing, eh, Miss Bella?"

"It does indeed, Mr. Kerswell, and an exciting one, too. I have never travelled on this stretch of the river before. Shall we see the really big ships close to, do you imagine?"

"If you wish it, then I am certain it can be arranged," replied Peter gallantly. "What do you say, Miranda?"

"Certainly," agreed Miranda. "Let us make the most of our opportunities and enjoy all the interests. Lord Oxenham is most knowledgeable about things nautical, perhaps he will be kind enough to be our tutor on such matters. Oh, but where has he gone?"

Oxenham had turned his back on the group and was striding towards the foundry gates, his face dark with discontent. It was bad enough being ignored, but what rankled most was the fact that he alone out of the gathering had not been asked his opinion about the proposed trip, it had been organized with no regard to him whatsoever. Worse still, he had not even been invited to be a member of the boarding party. His lordship was sulking!

"My lord!" Miranda caught up with him just before he reached the road. "My lord, you cannot be thinking of leaving us? We will be in a pretty pickle if you do, for we are relying upon you to keep us informed about all the shipping that we will see. It promises to be very interesting, and you know that you will enjoy it."

This was scarcely the sort of invitation to which Lord Oxenham was accustomed. For two pins he would have given this plain young lady one of the savage set-downs for which he was famous, the only drawback was that she was right. He would enjoy an outing on the river. Half a dozen invitations for the rest of the day awaited him at home, but not one of them held so much appeal.

The phrasing of his pithy set-down was very much in his mind, so Oxenham was surprised to hear himself say, "I suggest Tower Stairs as our most convenient point of embarkation, do you not agree?"

It took some time for the small convoy of carriages to be assembled, their passengers to board, and for them then to make a steady progress back along Whitechapel Road, down the Minories, then to the Embankment by the Tower. More time was spent discussing the relative merits of sail or oars, then finally came the hiring of a suitable craft.

"Will this journey take me very long, Mr. Kerswell?" asked Miss Bella. "I am beginning to feel inordinately hungry."

"Bella!" The young lady's Mama was shocked at her admission of such human frailties, particularly since Lucy seemed quite happy to dine on love. However, Miranda took Bella's part.

"We have all had a long morning, I dare say we could all do with nourishment," she agreed. "What of you, Mr. Denley? What did you eat for breakfast?"

"A little gruel, made very thin, some wine and water—" Arnold Denley's voice faded away weakly.

"There, I thought as much. You are in need of sustenance."

"Where do you suggest we go? Some chop-house in Wapping, or does anyone know of a pleasant eating-place in Bermondsey?" demanded Lord Oxenham, to prove that there was still acid in his tongue.

"How about Greenwich?" suggested Peter. "There is a splendid inn by the river with a good cook and tolerable cellar."

The hungry faces in the group brightened visibly, all except Oxenham who felt honour bound to object to any proposal put forward by Peter Kerswell.

"That is in the opposite direction!" his lordship complained loudly.

"True, but it is a fascinating stretch of the river, with much history attached to it. Besides, the boatman might be persuaded to let you take charge of the craft,'' said Miranda, her face all innocence.

Oxenham struggled hard to maintain his opposition to the scheme, but already the crew was manoeuvring the wherry in to the Stairs to take on the passengers. He could smell the tar and new hemp. The sails caught the breeze and cracked seductively. Lord Oxenham was seduced. They all went to Greenwich.

Peter's inn was everything he had promised. They dined leisurely and well, Arnold Denley in particular benefiting from the good cooking. Miss Branscombe had told him he needed nourishment, so he was determined to heed her advice, partaking only such dishes as had her expressed approval. With her encouragement he tucked away a slice or two of good lean ham, a small portion of salmon, a dish of coddled eggs and some baked pears. Declaring himself to be incredibly revived he allowed Miranda to tuck him up on a sheltered corner of the boat and proceeded to fall asleep.

"I have never seen my Cousin Denley look so well," commented Peter in a whisper. "Mark my word, Miranda, if you had the managing of him you would make him over into a veritable Hercules."

"I fancy that would be a rare bit of making over," smiled Miranda. "But he does look better, does he not? He even has some colour in his cheeks. However, I am not inclined to change my mind, I have no fancy for Mr. Denley as a husband, if he turns into Hercules or remains as he is."

"You do seem very definite on that point, so I must be content." Peter pretended to sigh. "I must say, this is a splendid notion of yours, sailing on the river. Something tells me you had it in your mind all along."

"In truth, I have wanted to do it for a long time. One learns so much about London from this vantage-point, but you know what it is like during the Season, never any time to do what one really wishes."

"So Cousin Denley provided an excellent opportunity."

"He did indeed, though I am sorry he was so poorly."

"I should not be too sorry, he seems to enjoy ill health, particularly when you are by."

"As a matchmaker you have at least the virtue of persistence."

"Which is only exceeded by your persistence in turning down my suggestions." Peter's eye fell upon Lord Oxenham, who was sitting at the tiller trying to look bored but failing abominably. "Here is one more suggestion which I fear you will turn down. I hope we are not going to be too often in the company of that Oxenham fellow. There is so much in his reputation that I do not like at all."

"Oh, Peter, when has he behaved at all objectionably in our presence?"

"It is what I hear of his activities in our absence that worries me."

"You are certain your hostility has nothing to do with the long talk he was having with Miss Bella on the journey from Tower Stairs?"

"Quite certain." Peter's face suddenly broadened into a grin. "For one thing I overheard much of what was said, and do you know the subject of the conversation? The types of rigging employed by the vessels in St. Katherine's Dock. Not Miss Bella's meat at all. She confided to me later that she was sadly disappointed in his lordship. She had heard so much about him that had put her on her guard, but apparently no one had warned her against him boring her to death."

"Which is exactly what I was saying. I am sure his reputation far outstrips the facts. Poor man, he is lonely and unhappy, anyone can see that."

"Only someone as charitable as you."

It was as well that their conversation was interrupted at this point, for Lord Oxenham had been an unwilling and aggrieved eavesdropper for several minutes. Aggrieved mainly at the loss of his reputation. Boring? Lonely? Unhappy? What epithets were these to describe the wicked Lord Oxenham, the very hint of whose exploits had been enough to send shivers of shock and delight down the spine of every proper young lady? Until now he had never doubted that he was irresistible to the opposite sex. Had not women fought over him? Pursued him? Hidden themselves in his house and even disguised themselves as servants just to gain admittance into his presence? Yet all this incredible attraction had been reduced in the course of one day to a lonely, unhappy man who was boring into the bargain! He was not just aggrieved, he was furious! He knew exactly where to lay the blame for this blemishing of his character. Miranda Branscombe! The only woman who had ever pitied him! He looked at her now, gawky and plain, quite unconcerned that the wind had blown her bonnet grotesquely askew. He could not understand how he had allowed her to inveigle him into such madcap schemes as sailing on the river or visiting Whitechapel in company with people of little wit and no fashion above the ordinary. Novelty, that was at the root of it. He had never known any female so ill-looking as she, and her total lack of flirtatiousness had been quite refreshing for a while, but for her to consider him lonely and unhappy was taking things too far. The novelty had worn off. He would drop the association at once. Being Oxenham he did not consider that any explanation would be necessary. Poor girl, she should count herself lucky to have spent so long in his company at all.

With such thoughts bolstering up his wounded pride Lord Oxenham handed the tiller back to the wherryman, assumed the haughty yet melancholy manner that was the delight of his female admirers and boded ill for his servants, and made only monosyllabic contributions to the conversation for the remainder of the journey.

Miranda had little opportunity to notice his lordship's change of mood, for Arnold Denley had woken up. In spite of great concentration on his part he found that he could not summon up a single ill, such a rare situation that he felt quite put about until he hit upon the happy notion of acquiring a morbid fear of drowning which occupied him most pleasantly until they reached York Stairs where their carriages were to await them. His newly found terror solicited much calming reassurance from Miss Branscombe, which was even more satisfactory than the fear itself. With much talk of the improvements in modern seamanship and the benefits of cork waistcoats she was able to keep Denley splendidly entertained.

Once on dry land Miranda was so engrossed in seeing Mr. Denley comfortably installed in his coach that she did not notice Lord Oxenham stride away to his own conveyance. This was the final straw to his lordship's sorely tried pride. Miranda Branscombe could at least have shown some distress at being so ignored by him. Oxenham rapped on the carriage roof and instructed his coachman not to be a confounded laggard. He was in a desperate hurry to get away from such an extraordinary, unnatural woman.

"His lordship has gone?" enquired this unfeeling creature of Mrs. Wordsworth-Pugh.

"But a minute ago, I believe, Miss Branscombe." Even this sharp-eyed lady had missed the fact that Lord Oxenham was put out about something, for Mrs. Wordsworth-Pugh's attention had been devoted to her daughter, Lucy, and Richard Branscombe. The pair had been inseparable all day, and only the most dull-brained person could have failed to notice the love that hung about them like a shining aura. There was one possible hindrance to their happiness, though, and Mrs. Wordsworth-Pugh decided to face it early.

"They make a pretty pair, do they not, your brother and my Lucy?" she remarked fondly, gazing to where Richard was bidding *au revoir* to his loved one whilst at the same time trying to hide the fact that he was holding her hand.

Miranda, too, looked in their direction and smiled.

"They certainly do. With Richard so dark and Miss Lucy so fair I fancy they would make perfect Dresden figures, both being so neat and trim."

Mrs. Wordsworth-Pugh beamed and concealed the tiniest sigh of maternal relief. Lowly ancestry and a fortune rooted in the corset industry could be terrible drawbacks to a girl in society, no matter how pretty or how much in love. Old families like the Branscombes could be very difficult upon such matters. Mrs. Wordsworth-Pugh knew her own powers of persuasion; she was confident she could bring Sir Henry to approve the match, but she had been less sure about Miranda. There was more under Miss Branscombe's bonnet than hair. Moreover, she was excessively fond of her brother and held a deal of influence over him. However, by her remarks she did not seem to disapprove of the alliance. Mrs. Wordsworth-Pugh warmed to her. Things were turning out to be most satisfactory. After all, if she could ensnare one male Branscombe for her family, why not two? Sir Henry was

still an excessively handsome man. Mrs. Wordsworth-Pugh permitted her heart to flutter and her
plumes to tremble a little on her own account before
she said, "I hope that I can persuade you and the
other members of your family to dine with us soon,
Miss Branscombe?"

"That will be delightful. I am sure we will all look
forward to receiving your invitation," answered Miranda.

"And perhaps Mr. Kerswell, too?"

Miranda looked in Peter's direction. He was helping Miss Bella into the carriage and taking a great deal
of time about it.

"Oh, and Mr. Kerswell, too," agreed Miranda with
the utmost confidence.

"I have every expectation of making a match of it
between Lucy and young Mr. Branscombe," Mrs.
Wordsworth-Pugh confided in her elder daughter once
they were back in the comfortable privacy of their
home in Great Brook Street.

"I hope you do. Although she has only known him
two minutes Lucy is so moonstruck over him she is
making an absolute cake of herself," replied Bella
frankly.

"I do wish you would not use those vulgar expression, my love," her mother admonished her. "Yes, to
have one daughter as the future Lady Branscombe will
be most satisfactory, particularly since he is such an
engaging young man, and so handsome. Mind you, I

am not sure but that you would be the better match for him.''

"Oh la, Mama, I do not care a fig if Lucy is wed before me, even though I am the elder by a year.''

"That is very generous-hearted of you, my darling," beamed Mrs. Wordsworth-Pugh. "But I was referring more to matters of temperament sooner than precedence. Lucy is such a mild little thing, and though Mr. Branscombe is perfectly charming he is not exactly a forceful character, is he? If you married him you could manage him very nicely.''

"What, and have Lucy hate me for the rest of my life? No thank you, Mama. Besides, if the truth were known I find the gentleman just a little milk and water. I prefer a suitor with more spirit.''

"Well, I will utter a small warning. Knowing how you like your own way in all things you will not get it with Mr. Kerswell, for all his cheery ways. If you have set your heart on him he will prove harder to catch than Richard Branscombe, mark my words. Still, perhaps things are best left as they are. Miss Miranda is sure to set up home with Lucy and dear Branscombe, for what else can she do, poor plain creature left upon the shelf as she is? She will doubtless see to their household for them, and she is so sensible and pleasant. Why, I dote upon her already.''

Mrs. Wordsworth-Pugh would have been most surprised to learn that at that very moment someone was harbouring most uncharitable thoughts about the lady she had just described so agreeably. Alone apart from two score of servants, in the empty cavern of his town residence, Lord Oxenham was finding any thoughts about Miranda Branscombe surprisingly painful. She had wounded his pride by pitying him, which no woman had ever done since he had begun to shave. What was worse, she was such a dowd! To have been treated thus by some proud beauty would have been supportable—almost!

I will not be regarded so by such a creature! No! Not ever! I will cut her dead should she cross my path! I will never acknowledge that we have even met! No word will we have exchanged, no not by my admission! I will teach the plain, inelegant female that she cannot behave so by me! And working himself into a rare tantrum his lordship hurled a valuable Venetian decanter at the wall, smashing it to smithereens and liberally baptizing a terrified and bewildered footman in a shower of the best Madeira.

CHAPTER SIX

UNFORTUNATELY for Lord Oxenham's punitive intentions Miranda did not even notice that she was being slighted. True, she had had no word from his lordship since the day of the boating expedition, but then she had never expected one. Why should Lord Oxenham wish to see her again when he had so many other fascinating pursuits to enjoy? Miranda happily continued with her own interests, interspersed with periods of playing hostess for her father, with no serious expectation of ever seeing Oxenham again.

The weather continued to be delightful, drawing hordes of the fashionable into the leafy shade of Hyde Park.

"With so many people about we are certain to meet someone we know," remarked Richard, as he strolled in the park with Miranda and Peter. "I wonder if Mrs. Wordsworth-Pugh and her daughters might decide to take an airing?"

His companion exchanged glances over his head.

"I hope you do not intend us to circuit the place until we do," said Peter. "After all, it is but three days since we last saw them."

"Three days? It must be more than that! It seems like an age, time drags so abominably slowly." Poor Richard had abandoned all reticence and was behaving like a typically anguish-torn lover.

"For myself I find that the hours speed by, but I can see how it must be very tedious for you, dear," Miranda consoled him.

"Could you not invite them to dine?" Richard pleaded.

"That would not be the thing," replied Miranda. "They dined with us not long since, so it is only polite to allow Mrs. Wordsworth-Pugh time to return our invitation. No, my dear, I have every sympathy with your anxiety to see the young lady again but the proprieties must be observed," she said firmly. Then as Richard heaved an agonized sigh she added gently, "But could you not make some contact with Miss Lucy? You could not have her to dine, not at a bachelor establishment, but you could perhaps send her some flowers."

"Would that be in order?" Richard's face began to brighten.

"I think so, if your bouquet is not too flamboyant and your message simple. You could send an accompanying note to Mama Wordsworth-Pugh asking her permission. I doubt if she would refuse."

"That is a splendid idea!" cried Richard. "What shall I send? A posy of summer flowers, all sweetly scented? Or maybe apricot rose-buds in a white holder—or gold? Pray will you both excuse me if I go to the florist's instanter?''

"Never let it be said that we stood in the way of true love," declared Peter with a flourish. "In such a public place I am confident that I may be alone with Miranda without compromising my reputation irretrievably."

"Oh!" Richard hesitated, uncertain whether or not his departure would be correct, then he caught sight of Peter's grin and his own features relaxed. "Oh, you are roasting me again! You catch me at every turn!" And with a happy smile he hurried away.

"Young Cupid was on form when he shot at your brother right enough," said Peter, as he and Miranda resumed their stroll.

"I fear so. As acute a case of love as I have ever seen. Thank goodness Miss Lucy seems to return his feelings. It would be dreadful if all the affection was on one side."

"You do not object to the match, then? Your ancient Branscombe blood does not recoil at the lady's lack of breeding?"

"Not if she genuinely loves Richard and will make him happy. But is it not ungallant of you to mention the Wordsworth-Pughs' lowly ancestry, particularly since you seem to be gazing in that direction yourself?"

"You forget, we Kerswells are *nouveau-riche*, the merest cits, in fact. It gives us much more scope in the marriage market, not having to bother with lineage and family-trees."

"Mrs. Wordsworth-Pugh will be relieved to hear that. She would be foolish not to be considering one daughter settled at Branscombe Hall, and I fancy she also has hopes of another at New Park. I would not be at all surprised if she enlists my help to achieve it."

"You do not need to concern yourself with arranging any match for me. I am more than capable of shifting for myself. Matchmaking is quite my forte, which is why I have taken yours in hand."

"Oh dear, you had not mentioned it for quite four-and-twenty hours. I had hoped you had given up that scheme."

"Given it up? Indeed not! The Kerswell dogged-ness has been at your disposal these two months. A husband shall be yours before the year is out."

"No more Mr. Denleys, I beg you."

"Your entreaties shall be heeded. I am only glad that my own were taken note of, for once."

"A strange statement. To what are you referring?"

"Why, to Lord Oxenham, of course. I am glad you have seen no more of him. He is an acquaintance who can do you no good."

"Are our acquaintances supposed to do us good?"

"Perhaps not, but nor are they supposed to do us harm, and that is what Oxenham would do to you."

"Oh Peter, you do not imagine that my virtue was at risk from him, who has all the beauties of London at his feet?"

"I know you are far too sensible for that, but you are also tender-hearted to an extreme degree. I could see your affections being engaged by such a man and that could only lead to pain for you. I do not trust him."

"Your opinion of Lord Oxenham's character is only slightly lower than your impression of my gullibility, seemingly," retorted Miranda.

"He is a selfish sort of cove, one who would be up to tricks for his own amusement. It would not trouble him if someone else got hurt."

Miranda was silent for a moment. She had to admit that similar thoughts had flitted briefly through her own head, but then she had been deeply ashamed to have harboured such uncharitable ideas.

"You do not believe that he was merely seeking some relief from constant boredom and flattery?" she asked at length.

"About as much as I believe in flying pigs and fairy gold. If you should meet Oxenham again, I beg you, do not pursue the acquaintance. I know you, you would try to redeem him or something, and the fellow is too much of a libertine for you to tangle with. There are tales—reliable tales—I could tell, only that they are not fit for your ears. Some of them put me to the blush."

"Which does not stop you from listening, I notice," Miranda observed tartly.

"I would have to be deaf not to hear some of them. There is not a week goes by but the clack in the coffee-houses is over some new scandal concerning him. I beg you not to acknowledge him any more."

"Because of coffee-house tittle-tattle? Certainly not!"

"You are being unusually obstinate. It will be the devil of a job to find you any prospective husband with Oxenham's shadow hanging over you."

"If they are all like Mr. Denley then I shall not be sorry."

"Take heed of what I say, do not see him again," Peter declared.

"The matter is purely academic, I am afraid," replied Miranda. "Lord Oxenham is walking towards us at this very minute. We cannot help but meet him."

"Cut him dead!" implored Peter.

He would have been surprised to have learnt that his lordship's thoughts were running on similar lines. Kerswell he would be happy to ignore, he had disliked the fellow from the start, but his full animosity was levelled at Miranda for having lured him into a situation where he had been accused of being boring, and then of having the audacity to pity him. It rankled still, and he raised his magnificent profile a fraction, so that Miss Branscombe would get the full benefit of the slight as he passed.

It was a waste of time. Miss Branscombe found it difficult to put the worst interpretation upon anyone's actions. She merely thought he had been temporarily blinded by the sun.

"Good morning, my lord. Is this not a beautiful day?" she said, totally ignoring Peter's beseeching. "I am glad that we met, for I have discovered something which I fancy might interest you. Have you decided upon a figure-head for your yacht?"

Lord Oxenham was determined to ignore the woman, all of his concentration was focussed to that end, so why then did his footsteps falter? Hang it all, why did the wretched female always manage to hit upon something that caught his attention? How did she know that the question of a figure-head had been occupying his brain of late? If she broached the subject then she was bound to have something specific in mind, he had learnt that much. His lordship came to a halt. He could slight her upon some other occasion.

"Your servant, Miss Branscombe. Mr. Kerswell." The bows exchanged by the two men were so slight as to be almost non-existent.

"A figure-head, my lord. Have you had thoughts upon the subject?"

"I have given the matter some attention, but by and large I think I shall decide against one. The garish caricatures I see nailed to the bows of most vessels are sadly wanting in refinement." Oxenham kept his voice cold and haughty.

"I agree, but what if you found something truly artistic and of real beauty? Would that not change your mind?" Miranda rummaged in a reticule that was twice the size of anything demanded by fashion and stuffed to bursting-point. "My enquiry is not an idle one. You see I have discovered a young wood-carver, a friend of Mr. Spiro, who is a man of exceeding talent. He was kind enough to show me some of his work, and among his exhibits there was one that struck me immediately as being ideal for your yacht. Even the subject was most appropriate—a nereid, a sea-nymph. Mr. Watts, the wood-carver, obligingly did a sketch for me, and I have it about me somewhere. Ah, here it is!''

Lord Oxenham took the crumpled paper from her between a fastidious finger and thumb. This was an excellent opportunity to snub Miss Branscombe by scorning the design.

"Oh really—'' he began contemptuously, then he was rash enough to glance at the sketch and his contempt turned into a tingle of excitement. It was exactly what he had been seeking—a sea-nymph leaning into the waves, her flowing locks and the soft folds of her draperies mingling with the foam. Every line of her, from her outstretched arm to the tip of each wreathing curl, seemed to dance upon unseen waves, and to embrace the far horizon. She was alive and eager to breast mountainous seas or to cleave her way through uncharted oceans. This nereid cried out to adorn the prow of some magnificent ship. His ship!

"I can promise you the craftsmanship is every bit as good as the design,'' said Miranda, noting the rapt expression on his face.

Belatedly Oxenham remembered all his disapproving intentions. They were going to be deuced hard to maintain.

"I would not have it coloured!" was the only objection he could muster.

"Certainly not," agreed Miranda. "The original was of unadorned applewood and no more than two feet high, but Mr. Watts assures me he could reproduce it in a greater size without loss of proportion or detail. Do you think that to have it totally gilded might be agreeable?"

"If it were true gilding and none of this tawdry yellow paint that is so much in vogue at the moment— Yes, and with gilded gingerbread work—a moderate amount—leading into a gold line to run the length of the hull. Indeed, I think that such a notion might prove most tasteful. Watts, you say this fellow is called? Have you his address about you? I shall certainly call upon him, and if his skill is as good as you say then I shall seriously consider commissioning him to do me a figure-head." His interest totally captured, Oxenham had forgotten all his uncharitable thoughts about Miranda, and he walked along by her side, looking at the sketch and discussing possible modifications.

Peter followed behind, a sullen, fuming addition to the group. His dislike and mistrust of Oxenham deepened, and for two pins he would have stalked off and left them; only, that would have abandoned Miranda into the clutches of the libertine lord. He had to be on hand to save her from Oxenham. What was more disturbing was his increasing fear that he might be obliged to save her from herself.

The sooner we find a husband for her the better! he grumbled silently. We must increase our efforts, Richard and I, and if I cannot get Richard's mind off his own matrimonial plans then I will continue the hunt by myself. Anything to get her away from Oxenham.

Peter's plans received a prompt set-back, for at that very moment Lord Oxenham was requesting Miranda to accompany him to the wood-carver's studio on the following day.

"You know the fellow, Miss Branscombe, and you seem to have the knack of talking to these people," Oxenham was saying. "I would take it as a kindness if you would come."

"What is the matter, does the fellow not speak English?" demanded Peter.

"I presume he does, though no doubt imperfectly." Oxenham shot him an icy glare. "However, I am not at ease when speaking to the lower orders, other than servants, and I want there to be no mistake in the understanding of my wishes."

"I dare say the lower orders will get the gist of your lordship's requirements if you speak slowly and raise your voice. Just imagine you are speaking to your dog," retorted Peter.

"I am obliged for your advice, Mr. Kerswell. I am sure you are more accustomed to such conversations than I," replied Oxenham smoothly.

"I am convinced that your lordship would feel at home in whatever level of society he found himself, even the very lowest," replied Peter. "However, just in case there are any problems I think I will come along too, if I may. I am eager to encourage anything that will complete your lordship's yacht swiftly and so speed you on your voyage."

"That is very kind of you, Peter," broke in Miranda, interrupting this dubious exchange before it got any further. "I dare say you will find it vastly interesting."

"Yes, I dare say you will, Mr. Kerswell. They tell me that wood-carving is one of the earliest forms of art, much appreciated by uncivilized aborigines. I am convinced you will find Mr. Watts' work very edifying." Pleased with this parting shot Lord Oxenham said his farewells and left before Peter could recover his breath.

It was only as he walked away that his lordship remembered his earlier resolution to cut Miranda dead. Ah well, it was too late to do anything about that now. He did not know what it was about Miranda Branscombe that he found so diverting, she was not witty and she was certainly not a beauty, yet somehow she always managed to keep him amused. It was quite extraordinary. Oxenham could look forward to a morrow devoid of boredom, a pleasing prospect. True, he would have to put up with Kerswell, and no doubt that doll-like brother of hers would come along too, but an entire day without its crosses to bear would be too much to ask. Oxenham's step was light as he crossed the park, and he even condescended to raise his hat to a stout matron and her family of dull lumpy daughters, causing them to reach for their vinaigrettes at being acknowledged by anyone so terribly and delightfully wicked.

Peter's mood, on the other hand, was far darker. He grumbled ceaselessly at Miranda about her folly in accepting Oxenham's invitation; and his humour was not improved by the return of Richard, who was smelling of April and May after dispatching his posy to Miss Lucy.

"Well, do not be in such a pet about it," Richard said upon being told of the next day's arrangements. "It is bound to be more comfortable than the visit to the foundry—wood-carving is a very clean occupation I believe, so I dare say it will not be above half disagreeable. Now, as I was telling you, the florist was most helpful and between us we devised the sweetest nosegay of lemon roses set in the most elegant ivory holder threaded with green ribbon. It is the prettiest thing I have seen, though still not pretty enough for Miss Lucy. She will have it within the hour. Oh, and as I was coming out of the shop I met Mr. Denley. He asked most kindly after you, Miranda. You do not think that after all—"

"No, I do not!" said Miranda gently but firmly.

"Ah well, it was but a thought. He was most interested in my sending a posy. I should not be at all surprised if he sent one to you, Miranda."

"That would be most kind of him, but I still do not want to marry him," said his sister.

"No wonder we are having little success in finding you a husband if you are so difficult to please," grumbled Peter.

"You sound out of sorts. Is something wrong?" asked Richard, surprised at his friend's unusual surliness.

"Lord Oxenham has given him a fit of the glooms," said Miranda.

"Oh, is that all. Well, do not despair, the Season is not over yet. I am sure we will find someone for Miranda," replied Richard cheerfully.

"Not with Oxenham hanging over us like a black cloud," muttered Peter. But Richard did not hear him. He was too busy describing to Miranda the letter he had sent to Mrs. Wordsworth-Pugh in company with Miss Lucy's posy.

BACK IN CAVENDISH SQUARE Sir Henry Branscombe had returned from an exhausting morning with his shirt-maker. Indeed, he found the entire Season wearing, with its round of tailors, hatters and the like, for he was obliged to give such affairs his entire attention. This morning, however, he had seen something which had raised his spirits considerably. As he had crossed the park he had noticed Miranda walking with

Lord Oxenham, and very close they had looked, talking away nineteen to the dozen. True, there was something havey-cavey about the fellow's reputation, but he was a lord, unmarried and his coat had been the best fitting Sir Henry had ever seen. The slam of the front door and heavy footsteps across the hall told him that Miranda was home. A few minutes later she entered the withdrawing-room, her eyes bright from exertion, her hair blown into rats' tails by the breeze.

"Hullo, Papa. Have you had an agreeable morning?" She bent and kissed him fondly, totally ignoring the censorious look he was giving to her dishevelled *coiffure*. "There was a note on the hall-table from Mrs. Wordsworth-Pugh. She wants us to dine at Great Brook Street on Thursday. She is certain to have sent an invitation to St. James's Street too, so Richard will be relieved, he has been waiting on tenterhooks to hear from her."

"It will make an entertaining evening, I suppose. Mrs. Wordsworth-Pugh is a near enough tolerable woman if one don't look at the top of her head, and her girls are beauties. Last time I saw Miss Lucy she was wearing a spotted silk that must have cost three guineas a yard, and I noted that her gloves matched her fan and her sash exactly. I like to see such attention to detail in a young lady."

"You must repeat that to Richard, he cannot hear too much approval of Miss Lucy," laughed Miranda, who was quite unaware that her blue bonnet and pink gloves did nothing to enhance the brown-and-rust striped poplin of her own gown.

"And how have you spent your morning, my dear?" asked her father, eager to take his mind off his daughter's sartorial disasters. "Was that Oxenham I saw you with in the Park?"

"Yes, it was. We met by chance, but I was pleased to see him, for I have found just the right figure-head for his yacht."

Sir Henry was not convinced that accessories for yachting were the normal province for young ladies, but even he could not hope that Miranda had kept silent about her discovery.

"Was his lordship pleased?"

"Yes, delighted. We are going to see it tomorrow. Now, if you will excuse me I must reply to Mrs. Wordsworth-Pugh."

"Yes, of course. Oh, before you go, some flowers came for you but the wretched florist has bungled the order. You had best sort it out. Banks has put them on the small table."

Miranda looked towards the table and saw a vase filled with white lilies, dignified and funereal in their purity. She began to laugh as she opened the accompanying note.

"I think I can guess—yes, I am right. They are from Mr. Denley, so there has been no mistake. That makes two letters to claim my attention."

Still laughing Miranda gathered up her lilies and left the room. Her father watched her go speculatively.

Lord Oxenham and Mr. Denley! Could it be that Miranda's style of plainness was coming into fashion? If so Sir Henry had not heard of it, but with two gentlemen claiming his daughter's time and attention it might be so. His heart lightened. Perhaps this Season would not end as disastrously as its five predecessors after all, at least as far as Miranda was concerned. As for himself, he still had to avoid the clutches of Mrs. Wordsworth-Pugh.

CHAPTER SEVEN

THE WEEKS PASSED and the London Season grew more and more frenzied. Much to his own surprise Lord Oxenham continued to see Miranda frequently. A dozen times he promised himself that he would break off the association, for she was not at all the sort of female for his tastes, and he was making a laughing-stock of himself by being seen with such an odd crea-ture, but just as frequently Miranda would bring something of interest to his attention or go off on some quest so intriguing that he could not resist fol-lowing. Demonstrations of electricity, and Mesmer-ism, parachute descents from balloons, performances by Joe Grimaldi—nothing was beyond the reach of her curiosity, and her enthusiasm drew Oxenham along in her wake. Not that she was one of those bus-tling, managing females. Far from it. For all her many activities Miranda Branscombe invariably exuded an air of quiet capability that was unusually restful.

As an antidote to what he feared might be the re-deeming influence of Miss Branscombe Oxenham pe-riodically reverted to his old haunts. The gaming-hells and bawdy-houses welcomed him as eagerly as be-fore, and in the fashionable *salons* of the *haute ton* he still reigned supreme—and he found it all boring beyond belief. Only with Miranda did he feel enthusiastic about anything, yet she never fawned upon him or showed the least sign of swooning at his feet—which considering the lady's size was probably just as well. Lord Oxenham went through that London Season a very perplexed man.

If Lord Oxenham was puzzled at his own behaviour then London in general was astounded. For weeks at a time his lordship committed no action worthy of the slightest gossip, and the lady in whose company he was most frequently seen proved to be of such spotless character that even the most persistent scribbler could not scrape up enough material about her to make a single line of print. More than one newspaper editor prayed nightly that this new surge of virtue would not catch on, else it would be the ruin of the entire industry.

In Miranda's own family Sir Henry was delighted by his daughter's friend, if very much in awe of the man himself. As for Richard, he confided in his beloved Lucy, "Oxenham seems quite taken up with Miranda, and I am glad, for her sake. He seems an excellent genteel fellow."

"If you approve of him then I am sure he must be a very worthy gentleman," Lucy had replied, too much in love and far too uncritical of her inamorato to realize that his judgment of character was non-existent.

Only Peter did not approve.

"This association will lead to nothing but trouble. How are we to find a husband for Miranda with Oxenham always in her pocket?" was his constant cry, but no one heeded him. The result was that he became frequently ill-humoured, an uncommon state of affairs with him, and he had the greatest difficulty in making himself civil to anyone, even Miss Bella.

"It is kind of you to worry about me so," Miranda said, "but I fear you are upsetting yourself to no purpose. My friendship with Lord Oxenham is of the most platonic nature, and you cannot tell me you do not believe in such a thing for you and I have been friends for goodness knows how long."

"But our situation is quite different. We have known each other since cradle days, and I am as fond of you as if you were my sister—no, dash it, fonder than that, for I do not like some of my sisters above half. Besides, I know I am no saint, but my reputation would require a deal of working at before it is anywhere near as black as Oxenham's."

"Now you are singing an old song," Miranda chided him gently. "I am firmly convinced that poor Lord Oxenham is more sinned against than sinning. Too many people are prepared to think the worst of him."

"Well, count me among the latter, and I declare that if he harms you I shall call him out."

"Oh, promise me that you would never do anything so foolish!" Miranda was quite alarmed. "You know my virtue is in no danger. Can you not see that

I am just something of a novelty to the man? And, poor fellow, he is sadly short of novelty. It must be a sorry plight, to have everything one desires at too early an age—wealth, position, genius.''

"It has not spoilt me at all so why should it affect him?'' declared Peter gravely.

"Ah, but he lacks a clutch of elder sisters to help maintain his equilibrium,'' smiled Miranda, relieved that the conversation was gaining a light-hearted note.

"That is true. Life with my sister Sophia and the rest was baptism of fire enough to make a saint out of any man.''

"I thought you said just now that you were no saint,'' Miranda pointed out.

"A slip of the tongue, nothing more. Only modesty prevents me from pointing out my own manly perfection.''

"Hmm, I should save such speeches to impress Miss Bella.''

Peter laughed. "I should certainly save them for someone who knows me less thoroughly than you. But do not think you can divert the conversation away from Lord Oxenham and his imperfections.''

Miranda sighed. "Peter, I know you have my best interests at heart, but I beg of you, do not be too down on my friendship with him. It is so nice to really please Papa and Richard for once.''

"Sir Henry and Richard? How do they come into it?''

"You have suffered my other London Seasons along with me, you know how disastrous they were and how poor Papa suffered as a consequence. I am a sad disappointment to him. Even though he has always been the kindest, most affectionate of fathers I would be stupid not to realize how much more comfortable he would be with a daughter like Lucy Wordsworth-Pugh for example, someone pretty and elegant, someone who does not stick out like a sore thumb—a very large sore thumb. Now, because of Lord Oxenham's friendship I have received dozens of invitations that would otherwise never have come my way. I have been taken up by fashionable society at last. Why, I have even made being plain quite the thing, for I am sure that I notice far more plain females about than ever I did before—and Papa is delighted. For myself, I do not care a fig about being plain and awkward, but it does hurt Papa and Richard so, they are both so beautiful and graceful. I pray you, let us enjoy this Season while it lasts, it has not many weeks to run."

Peter was silent for a long while, and when he spoke his voice was very quiet.

"Miranda, I am a brute, I had not thought that I might be spoiling things for you. How typical of you to be more concerned for your father and brother than for yourself. I promise you, no more grumbling or threats to call Oxenham out. Mind you, I shall keep a firm eye on him to ensure that he behaves himself. Not even for your sake can I bring myself to like the man, but you shall enjoy what is left of your Season. As you say, it is almost over.''

''Yes, we shall all soon be leaving Town, and I doubt if I will ever see Lord Oxenham again.''

''Will you be sorry?''

''Certainly, I like him exceedingly. When he forgets to play the wicked lord or be the literary lion he is a most amiable companion and always worth listening to, for he has travelled so widely. Also, if I am honest, it is very pleasant to be the object of other females' envy just for once, even if they are as puzzled about it as I am. But I have no expectation of our relations going any further, I assure you. I shall be quite content to return to Branscombe Hall an old maid. In fact, I am looking forward to it. Richard and Lucy will undoubtedly get married, and I am relying upon them to provide me with lots of nephews and nieces to play with as soon as possible.''

''If you are so desperate for nephews and nieces then you can have some of mine,'' said Peter generously. ''I have enough and to spare, but I do not accept that you are resigned to spinsterhood. You are the dearest creature, and you deserve the finest, kindest husband in the land, and I intend to find him for you.''

Miranda's cheeks flushed at this compliment and her eyes were suddenly unusually bright.

''Now it is you who is being kind,'' she said. ''But I beg you, do not set yourself an impossible task, I know such a husband is not for me. Apart from all else, I would not have you neglect your own wooing in an attempt to marry me off. Miss Bella would not like it, and I fear her Mama would be miffed.''

"Never fear, Mrs. Wordsworth-Pugh is not likely to let me off the hook so lightly. I am thankful that at the moment her energies are concentrated upon landing Richard for Miss Lucy, though to be honest he seems more than willing to give himself up. No doubt Mrs. Wordsworth-Pugh will give me the benefit of her full attention in good time, and by then I have every hope of having found you a husband.''

"But no Mr. Denley," said Miranda, as he rose to say farewell.

"Very well, no Cousin Denley if you are so set on it, though I grow more and more convinced that we could bring him up to snuff with very little effort. Still, I shall just have to look elsewhere.'' And with a cheery wave Peter departed from Cavendish Square.

From her window Miranda watched him walk across the square, and as he reached the corner of Holles Street he turned and waved to her. She thought how handsome he was, almost as handsome as Richard. Mrs. Wordsworth-Pugh was going to have a pair of splendid sons-in-law. Peter disappeared from sight and Miranda made to turn back into the room, but another figure entering the square caught her eye. There was something depressingly familiar about that slight, fragile frame. Arnold Denley was heading in her direction. Worse still, he had seen her at the window so there was no escape.

A few minutes later Mr. Denley was announced. He entered the room, his face set in an expression of acute gloom.

"Miss Branscombe," he said. "I have come to bid you good-bye. Not *au revoir*, not even farewell, but a final and definite good-bye."

"You are returning to Somerset?" asked Miranda, ashamed at the sudden surge of relief that overwhelmed her.

"Alas, no, at least not ultimately. My destination is more permanent. I go to that final destination of us all. In short, my days are numbered."

A few months earlier such a speech would have filled Miranda with a deep and genuine compassion, but experience had taught her to temper sympathy with sense where Denley was concerned.

"How distressing. Are you certain?" she asked, looking at him steadily.

"Pretty certain." Denley began to fidget under her scrutiny. "Are you not the tiniest bit sorry for me? I was convinced that you, above all people, would be."

"If what you say is true then of course I will be sorry for you, but might you not be mistaken? Who gave you this opinion?"

"All of them. All of Harley Street—in a way."

"It seems peculiar tidings to be given 'in a way'. What did the doctors say exactly?"

"It was what they did *not* say. It can be the only conclusion."

"Mr. Denley," said Miranda, her gentle voice unusually firm, "please tell me the doctors' exact words."

Arnold Denley wriggled happily in his chair. This was really most satisfactory. Such a dramatic statement from him usually brought forth comments of sympathy that were patently insincere and born of total indifference. Only his dear departed Mama had ever been so insistent with him. Miss Branscombe was indeed a treasure.

"As you know I came to London with the intention of visiting Harley Street. I promised myself that I would get the opinions of the best medical men in the land, so I have worked my way up one side of the street and down the other, as far as Marylebone Street and back. This morning I visited the last one, a Doctor Baum who resides just round the corner from this very house. My dear lady, they are all baffled. My malady defies science."

"It does?" Miranda's voice was almost stern.

Denley wilted a little.

"They cannot agree," he said. "One puts the trouble at the fault of my liver, another at a disorder of the blood. One says I must fast constantly, another decrees a diet of red meat and porter. If I have so puzzled the medical minds of London there is only one thing left to do, return to my estates in Somerset and await the end."

"That wait could be a long one, another thirty or forty years," said Miranda briskly.

"You think so? So long?" Denley was quite shocked at such an idea. "But the best medical minds—"

"Were paid very handsomely by you for their services. Naturally each would wish to justify his fee. Since they disagree so radically has it not occurred to you that another interpretation could be put upon their hesitation—that nothing serious ails you?"

"Miss Branscombe!" Denley was quite affronted.

"Consider, Mr. Denley. You take a deal of physick every day, do you not? If I took a quarter of the potions and pills that you swallow I should feel most unwell indeed, and I know myself to be in excellent health. You admit these medicaments do you no good. Might it not be worth trying to abandon them altogether, for an experimental period at least?"

"Miss Branscombe!" cried Denley again, for her words spelt both blasphemy and revolution in one breath.

"Think on it. If you still feel ill after taking all your cures you have nothing to lose by dispensing with them."

"Entirely? Not even liver salts?"

"No."

"But surely a little digestive elixir?"

"Not even that."

"But I must do something. What do you suggest?"

"Do you know the occasion when I saw you in greatest health, Mr. Denley? The day of the river excursion, a day when you had had much fresh air and some good plain nourishment. Does that not tell you something?"

"I— I think so, but what if I have one of my giddy turns, or need some help? I will need someone, I really will." Excitement and terror were gripping Denley in turns at these extraordinary notions.

"Of course you will," agreed Miranda. "What you need is good genuine medical advice that is not influenced by how many guineas can be squeezed from your purse. I will give you the name of our own physician, or rather physicians, for they are a father and son in practice together. That way you gain the experience of the one and the modern ideas of the other. I suggest that you consult them immediately and put my ideas to them. I promise you they will not fill you with medicines needlessly."

"You really think it is worth trying?"

"Do not you? Or would you prefer to return to Somerset, there to await your demise?"

Denley looked thoughtfully at Miranda. A salutary thought had just occurred to him. If his days were numbered then it would scarcely be worth while making Miss Branscombe his wife, would it? Embarking upon matrimony was a business fraught with nervous anguish, and he had no intention of going through all that for a mere month or two of marriage.

"It is worth it!" he cried. "Fresh air is what I need, and exercise and good plain food. I shall direct my cook the minute I get home. I shall walk in the park daily, and I shall ride, and there is fencing, I hear that is a very beneficial occupation. Who knows, when I have built up my strength a little I may encompass other sports. I may even go a few rounds with Tom Cribb."

"Who knows indeed?" agreed Miranda, a little startled by the enthusiasm she had engendered. "But I beg you take things slowly at first before embarking upon fisticuffs on such a scale, and do consult Doctor Lee and his son, who will advise you well."

"I shall, I shall. Oh Miss Branscombe, what a debt I owe you! I come to you a dying man and I leave you reborn."

"You are too generous," said Miranda, her alarm increasing. "I am only happy that you feel more optimistic."

"Optimistic? Miss Branscombe, I feel almost well already. A miracle, that is what it is! Now, if you will forgive me I must leave you. I am engaged to dine with Mrs. Wordsworth-Pugh and her charming daughters. I trust I shall see you there? I think I shall walk home. Yes, I shall definitely walk. It will be so invigorating." Happily absorbed by his redirected search for health Arnold Denley left a thankful and amused Miranda.

Miranda did indeed meet him again at the Wordsworth-Pugh's later that same day, but there was no chance for further talk of healthy diets and brisk exercise. Another topic of conversation stole everyone's attention, for that very day Richard had formally asked for the hand of his beautiful Lucy and had been accepted.

"I am quite beside myself with joy," declared a triumphant Mrs. Wordsworth-Pugh, victory quivering in every strand of her plumes. "Of course, some people might consider it gothic for Lucy to be settled before Bella, she being the younger, but I say why stand in the way of a true love-match merely for formality's sake. Besides, with my Bella's looks I fancy it will not be long before she is walking down the aisle too, eh, Mr. Kerswell?"

Peter bowed gallantly and replied, "It will be a lucky fellow who wins Miss Bella, ma'am."

"Are you sure you will not volunteer to be that lucky fellow?" whispered Miranda as Mrs. Wordsworth-Pugh left them.

"Volunteering is quite unnecessary when Mrs. W-P is about," grinned Peter. "I only hope that she is so pleased at collaring Richard she lets me finish the Season in peace."

"She has rather taken to the rôle of *belle mère*," agreed Miranda.

"Even to the point of offering to organize the refurbishing of Branscombe Hall. I thought poor Sir Henry would have an apoplexy when she suggested lilac print gowns for the maidservants and crimson coats for the men, and then went on to advocate yellow and lime-green silk hangings for the walls."

"Yes, poor Papa, he has a very sensitive eye for colour," chuckled Miranda, "but the good lady has not offered to refurbish me, at least not yet. She was kind enough to say how glad she was that I was part of Branscombe Hall, for I would be invaluable to Richard and Lucy in the years to come."

"That makes you sound like the fixtures and fittings," exclaimed Peter indignantly. "Like the fire-irons or the boot-scraper or something. Well, the lady will be disappointed for you will not be there for long. Your new husband will carry you away to a home of your own. Do not look like that! It will happen. Have I not said so? It is useless to rely on Richard now—all he does is sigh and talk of Lucy, so I must take entire charge myself. Indeed, I have already been active on your behalf. I have five or six excellent fellows all lined up for you."

"Where are they?" asked Miranda, craning her neck. "Or have I overlooked them in the crush at some point?"

"I shall introduce them one at a time and with the utmost propriety," said Peter with dignity.

He was as good as his word. Several worthy gentlemen were brought forward by him in the next few weeks, introduced to Miranda, then happily faded into obscurity again. Peter was puzzled and angry.

"What is wrong? Is not Miss Branscombe the nicest female a fellow could meet?" he demanded of one Major Percy Welbeck, late of His Majesty's Hussars.

"Of course she is, dear fellow. I cannot remember spending a more pleasant evening with a lady."

"Then why did you disappear so quickly? You need a wife, you told me so yourself, else your father is likely to cut your allowance, so what is wrong with Miranda? Is it that she is no beauty?"

"Good heavens, no!" Percy Welbeck looked indignant. "She is such a good sort I am sure I could have got used to that sooner or later. No, it is—"

"Go on!" insisted Peter.

"If you must know, I understand that Oxenham has been seen in the lady's company a great deal."

"So?"

"You know his reputation as well as I do. A dashed awkward devil when crossed. I have no wish to get in his bad books. Oh, think me a funk if you please. If my affections were truly engaged then it would be a different story, but they ain't, and if it is all the same to you I would sooner not provoke Oxenham's ire by snatching his lady friend from under his nose. He once horsewhipped a fellow for alienating his spaniel's affections. Think what he would do for a female!"

Welbeck was not alone. Surprisingly few gentlemen were willing to cross Oxenham's path. Peter groaned aloud. This was what he had feared. The trouble was he could not think of a way round the problem. All he could do was to pray for the end of the Season, when Oxenham's friendship with Miranda was bound to cease.

The heat and the airless state of London made many other people long for the end of the Season. All but the most dedicated Metropolitans were eager to get away to their country estates or to enjoy some sea air at one of the fashionable watering-places.

Lord Oxenham viewed this prospective change in the social scene with some dread. It went against the grain to admit that he enjoyed anything, but this Season had been far more entertaining than most. The thought of spending the ensuing months moving from place to place, a perpetual house-guest among people who welcomed him merely for the distinction of saying that they knew the wickedest lord in England, was not an attractive one. The thought of rattling about in the medieval vastness of his country seat was even worse. It occurred to Oxenham that he had no true friends. No one really cared for him. Only Miranda Branscombe had ever felt compassion for him, and offhand he could think of none other among his regular acquaintances who had ever suffered this emotion. If Miss Branscombe could be with him at that very moment then at least he would have some decent company and sensible conversation that did not depend upon the ceaseless, mindless tittle-tattle of Town. Yes, Miranda Branscombe would be the perfect antidote to his depression, but alas the lady was entertaining her brother's future in-laws to dinner, and not even Oxenham would gate-crash such a domestic gathering.

Bored in the extreme, his lordship was in the process of drinking more brandy than was good for him when his butler entered.

"What is it, Finch?" he demanded, angry at this intrusion into his misery.

"Lady Whitelea, my lord," announced Finch.

The words were scarcely out of his mouth before the lady herself entered the room, and with a cry of "Darling Oxenham" flung herself into his lordship's arms.

Slender, exquisitely beautiful, a perfect vision in soft rose-tinted gauze, Maria Whitelea had until recently been Oxenham's most constant companion, and the subject of more than one scandalous paragraph in the lower realms of the Press. Beautiful and witty, she had never allowed her marriage to an elderly Tory peer to interfere with her devotion to Oxenham, and now she demonstrated her affection most graphically.

In the past Oxenham would not have objected to such adoration, but simply accepted it as his due. Today, however, his irritability refused to be dispelled.

"Be more discreet, Maria," he grumbled. "Finch is scarcely out of the room."

Maria removed her arms from about his neck and looked at him, puzzled.

"When have you ever cared for the good opinion of Finch?" she demanded. "And anyway, by now he must surely know that we are desperately in love. What is the matter? I thought you would be pleased to see me."

"Of course I am pleased to see you," he snapped, in a voice that suggested otherwise. "It is just that I have spent a very boring day."

Maria looked at him quizzically.

"I am not surprised. I hear that you have taken up with the strangest set of country nobodies. Kitty Alphington says she saw you in Hyde Park with the oddest-looking creature about a mile high and wearing a frightful bonnet. What are you up to, Oxenham? Is this one of your pranks? If so, pray let me in on it."

"No, it is not a prank," growled his lordship. "And Miss Branscombe is merely somewhat on the tall side for a lady, not some giantess. I am surprised at you listening to Kitty Alphington, you know what a vicious gossip she is."

"My, how you spring to the lady's defence! That is not like you." Maria's voice had become waspish. "Ah, I see it all. She is a prodigious heiress and you have got yourself in the suds so you are obliged to dangle after her. My poor darling!"

Maria's pitying words, insincere as they were, irritated Oxenham even more.

"What nonsense! You know there is not a word of truth in it. Oh change the subject, for pity's sake! Can you think of nothing but gossip to repeat? Have you no conversation at all?" he demanded.

"You accuse me of having no conversation? I am boring you, am I?" Maria's temper was fraying now. "And what about my boredom? You have not been near me for an age. I have been waiting and waiting for some message from you, condemned to listen to Whitelea's ramblings until I thought I would scream. Yet you could not send me even a little note to inform me of your plans."

"There was no reason why I should. I had no appointment to see you that I recall, and I am not your husband, thank heaven!"

This last remark took Maria's breath away, a very temporary bereavement. When it returned she used it with great force.

"Oh!" she shrieked. "Oh, you ingrate! You monster! To speak to me so! You have no feelings, you are cold and hard and callous! How could I have been deceived into giving you my love? The sacrifices I have made for you, the risks I have taken! Poor Whitelea, if only he knew. If the whole world knew what we have been to each other these past years!"

"The whole world will know if you continue to bellow at that rate," interposed Oxenham irritably. "I suggest, madam, that you go and stand on Westminster Bridge and scream your indiscretions from there, it will give you a wider audience—and you are giving me a headache!"

This piece of candour was too much! Lady Whitelea gave a gasp, burst into tears and fled from the room. Angrily Oxenham stalked after her, only to be greeted by the slamming of the front door.

"Mallard!" bellowed his lordship at his valet, who was unfortunate enough to appear at that moment.

"Mallard, when I wed it must be to a female with a quiet voice, do you hear?"

"Yes, my lord," replied the valet, bemused.

"And she must be good-tempered and not boring! Above all else I must not be shackled to a boring female, do you understand?"

"Yes, my lord," repeated Mallard. This was not a good moment to confess that he was totally bewildered.

"And if she has not all three qualities, Mallard, you are to stand up in church and prevent the match! When the priest reaches that part about there being any just impediment you are to speak out, do you hear? For I shall hold you entirely responsible if I get myself tied to some screeching, dull-witted harridan. Have I made myself clear?"

"Yes, my lord," replied Mallard, without perfect truth.

"Very well. You may go."

Below stairs in the butler's quarters Mr. Finch was setting out two glasses and the decanter of sherry for the little nightcap he customarily shared with Mr. Mallard.

"My dear Mr. Mallard, what is the matter? You look quite done up," he said, as his friend entered the room.

"I have good reason, Mr. Finch. The strangest thing has occurred. His lordship has referred to his marriage."

Mr. Finch's lower lip quivered, the nearest thing to his jaw dropping that dignity would allow.

"His lordship said 'when I wed'," went on Mallard. "'When', mark you. Not 'if', and goodness knows I have only heard him mention the possibility of him ever marrying once in these last ten years!"

"Perhaps you did not hear aright," suggested the butler.

"There was no mistake about it. His lordship was very, very definite on the point. 'When I wed', he said, clear as a bell. I had no idea we were thinking of marriage, had you?" Mallard always identified most strongly with his employer.

"No indeed. Do we know any marriageable ladies?" replied Finch in the same vein.

"Plenty of beautiful ones, but marry any of them—" Mallard shook his head. "There is Miss Branscombe, of course, the lady there has been all the talk about. A very pleasant lady but terribly plain."

Both men shook their heads. Knowing his lordship's taste for lovely but highly dramatic women they sadly discarded Miss Branscombe.

"Such luck would not be ours," said Mr. Finch with regret. Without another word he replaced the sherry with a bottle of Lord Oxenham's finest cognac and poured each of them a generous measure. "Mr. Mallard, my friend," he said gravely, "things look serious for us, very serious indeed."

CHAPTER EIGHT

FASHIONABLE SOCIETY packed its bags and headed for cooler, more comfortable climes, leaving London shrouded in holland and drugget. As Miranda was bowled westwards in the Branscombe carriage she found that she was leaving Town with mixed emotions. It would be good to be home again, to walk through lush green grass and to smell the breeze fresh and salt-laden from the sea, but she would have been less than human if she had not experienced a pang of regret at leaving Lord Oxenham. She had genuinely liked him, and only a block of wood would have been insensible to the attentions of so attractive a man, but now all that was over. The Season was at an end and it was unlikely that she would ever see him again. Not that she had harboured any romantic notions; she had long since accepted that such dreams were for other, prettier girls, yet the interlude had been very pleasant. With the faintest of regretful sighs Miranda set her thoughts to a life returned to normal—though not quite normal, for Richard and Lucy's wedding loomed on the horizon.

Mrs. Wordsworth-Pugh had opted for an autumn wedding, and no one had the temerity to contradict her.

"It would be too, too cruel to part our love-birds until that Special Day, so I have taken a darling little house not a mile from the gates of Branscombe Hall. Is that not splendid?" declared that indefatigable lady in the same breath as she informed everyone that she had already booked the church, chosen the hymns, instructed the clergyman and had some strict words to say about the sermon.

Richard had been delighted to learn of the proximity of his loved one, but his father had been less happy. Sir Henry found the lady's choice of puce plumes, whatever the shade of her gown, too much to bear; besides, he was afraid he could interpret her intentions towards himself all too well. He was not against remarriage on principle, but marriage to those plumes!

"Did you say one mile, madam?" he asked hesitantly.

"Scarcely that, Sir Henry. After all, there is much in this region that I mean to keep my eye on." Mrs. Wordsworth-Pugh beamed coquettishly and fluttered her eyelashes, making sure that her gaze took in both Sir Henry and Peter.

"Tally-ho, the hunt is up!" the latter breathed in Miranda's ear. "I fancy it is open season for your Papa and me."

"I wonder you do not give in now and save everyone a lot of trouble," replied Miranda.

"There is one thing stopping me. I have a dread fear that Miss Bella could turn out to be like her mother given another ten or twenty years."

"What a fellow you are! Here you are promising to arrange my marriage, yet making a sorry muddle of your own affairs. I had quite looked forward to seeing you betrothed to Miss Bella any day now."

"It could come to that yet, but there is some run in me still. I might make it until Christmas."

"I do not think your Newmarket friends would give you very good odds."

"We shall see. The betting on your impending marriage would be very keen, though. I intend to give it my undivided attention from now on. If nothing else it should keep me out of the range of Mama Wordsworth-Pugh. Our chances are so much greater now that you have shaken off Oxenham."

"I do not approve of your choice of words," Miranda reproved him. "But I doubt if I will see his lordship again. He has probably forgotten all about me by now."

Miranda was wrong in her surmise. Oxenham had not forgotten her. In fact, it was amazing how often she crept unbidden into his thoughts. Anyone who can drive away my boredom is worth cultivating, he told himself, after suffering three interminable weeks on his own estate, and he began to ponder upon how he could meet her again.

Unfortunately, through lack of usage, Lord Oxenham had lost the knack of renewing the acquaintance of respectable females, and the problem gave him much food for thought. The answer came from an unexpected source. A letter from Mr. Bray, the ship-builder, giving a progress report on the new yacht, added that the sea-trials were to take place within the next two weeks, weather permitting. In one inspired sentence Mr. Bray had added, "Your lordship's presence at this stage would be most welcome, should your lordship feel inclined, so that your lordship might suggest further improvements and embellishments to the vessel."

His lordship did feel inclined. Oh, worthy Mr. Bray! Oxenham congratulated himself upon finding a craftsman of such superior intelligence.

He was not travelling all the way to Devon to see Miranda Branscombe! Upon that point Oxenham was very clear in his own mind. All the way down in his carriage he told himself that the sole purpose of his journey was to see his yacht, but with acquaintances in the neighbourhood it would be churlish not to visit. Which was why he was in the country a whole twelve hours before he presented himself at Branscombe Hall.

"My lord, this is an unlooked-for pleasure," said Miranda, genuine delight in her welcoming smile.

"I was in the district, madam—I have affairs to attend to—so as I was passing your gates I thought I would call," he replied curtly to quash any suspicions the lady might have that she was the reason for his presence.

But such a thought never entered Miranda's head. No gentleman would make even the slightest detour for her company.

"It must be your yacht that has brought you here!" she cried. "Oh, is she as you envisaged her? How does the figure-head look?"

Nothing loath, Oxenham answered her questions.

"She has exceeded my expectations in every way, and as for the figure-head, it has provided the ideal finishing touch. I understand that it has already been much admired by everyone who has visited Bray's yard. The only reservation I have about the vessel is in her ballast. I have a fancy she still may be too light in the water." Before he knew it Oxenham was engrossed in a detailed conversation about his new toy— the modification to the main cabin he had ordered, the difficulties over getting exactly the right suit of sails to please him. Miranda listened with enthusiasm, demanding to know the most minute detail.

"So you have not actually sailed in her yet, my lord?" she said at last.

"No, not yet, though I can scarcely contain my impatience. Her sea-trials are set for the day after tomorrow. Bray assures me that the weather is settled and the wind should remain in the right quarter, so I am confident that nothing will delay us. Perhaps you would care to accompany me on the trials. You have been kind enough to show a lively interest, it seems only right that you should share the experience. Oh, but you could not come alone, could you? That would not be proper. Very well, perhaps your father and your brother—and did I hear that Mrs. Wordsworth-Pugh and her family are in the neighbourhood? You cannot come without female companions." Oxenham listened to himself with disbelief. Had he not planned to be cool and distant towards Miss Branscombe? Yet here he was inviting not only her but half the boring provincial neighbourhood on board his precious yacht! "The conditions will be rather primitive. I cannot guarantee comfort," he added quickly, intending to countermand his rash invitation and put Miss Branscombe off, but oddly enough he found that he still wanted her to come. So much so that he was quite relieved when she replied, "I am sure we will all understand that it is to be a working-trip, and though I cannot speak for the others I must say that I shall be delighted to accept."

Oxenham was pleased. Miss Branscombe's presence would make all the difference, even if it meant being hampered by a whole tribe of chaperons. Chaperons! It had been years since he had considered such encumbrances to be necessary when he desired the company of a young lady! What was happening to him? Could he be suffering from the effects of creeping insanity, or worse still, middle-age?

Lord Oxenham left Branscombe Hall trying to persuade himself that the sea-trials would be the most frightful bore, yet at the same time keeping an anxious eye on the weather. He also proceeded to worry the life out of poor Mr. Bray, seeking assurances that the cloudless sky and light breezes would last for two more days.

"Oxenham is here? And taking you off to sea? He is up to no good!" declared Peter angrily when he heard of the day's events. "What he intends to do when he gets you on the high seas I dare not imagine!"

Miranda chuckled. "Your knowledge of life on a ship under full sail is obviously limited. Do you not realize that apart from the crew and our party there will also be a considerable number of Mr. Bray's workmen on board too? Such a multitude will leave scant opportunity for dark doings, I am thinking."

"You ought not to be thinking of dark doings at all, a well-brought-up young lady!" snapped Peter. "It is Oxenham's influence on you. But you are right when you say I know little of life on board ship. I only wish I knew less. I prefer my transport to be well provided with legs and to have at least some inkling of what I mean when I shout whoa! The sea is all very well, but it does not stay still."

"Then it is as well that you are not coming."

"I am not so certain. I am far from convinced that you will be properly looked after."

"Such nonsense! Richard will be there, and all three Wordsworth-Pugh ladies. Papa found that he had a prior engagement once he learnt that Mrs. Wordsworth-Pugh was to be of the party. I fancy he has decided to fight fire with fire where that lady is concerned, for I notice he has been paying marked attention to Captain Bakewell's pretty widow lately."

"A charming lady, and one whose taste in head-dresses is impeccable. I owe your father my apologies—he has far more cunning than I gave him credit for, but that still leaves you sadly unprotected. Richard will be gazing so deeply into Lucy's eyes he would not notice if the entire ship were overrun by pirates and you carried off by Blackbeard himself."

"I have never been carried off by a pirate—it might be an enlightening experience. Do you think we stand a chance of meeting some?" asked Miranda innocently.

"You are not taking me seriously, but if you did—meet some pirates, I mean—then I would wager my last farthing that Mama Wordsworth-Pugh would be running her eye over them to pick out any promising husband material, either for Miss Bella or for herself."

"You do not seem overtly concerned for Miss Bella's safety, I notice."

"She will be well guarded. I would back her Mama against all the pirates in the seven seas. And incidentally, even Mrs. Wordsworth-Pugh has discounted Oxenham as a suitable son-in-law, which should give you a serious hint as to that gentleman's reputation—or lack of it."

"I must say I am quite glad you are not coming. You would be the most frightful impediment to an otherwise very enjoyable day," replied Miranda evenly.

"Well, do not be too sure. Perhaps I should come after all, simply to guard your virtue."

Miranda laughed, not taking him seriously.

On the day appointed for the sea-trials she found herself waiting on the dockside at Mr. Bray's yard. Oxenham was not there to greet her, a piece of impoliteness he had deliberated on for some time that morning. It would not do for Miss Branscombe to think that he was over-eager for her company, therefore he would make her wait. The fact that he had been dressed and waiting in his rooms at the inn for a full hour before he set out, and that he had consulted his watch at least twelve times in that hour, was neither here nor there. It was as well that he never learnt that Miranda had merely put his tardy appearance down to her own early arrival. Richard, of course, was only interested in the coming of Lucy.

"They are devilish late. You do not think they have had an accident?" he asked anxiously.

"No, I do not. You were so eager to get here you ordered the carriage for a good half-hour earlier than was necessary, so you must expect to wait." Her fond tone took away any possible sharpness from her words. Love had smitten Richard so completely what could one do but treat him as some slightly ailing child?

Fortunately for Richard's peace of mind a carriage rumbled through the narrow entrance of the shipyard, and he rushed forward to help his beloved alight. Had the couch been otherwise totally empty he would have been quite content, but the vehicle proved to be well packed. After Lucy her Mama stepped down, followed by Miss Bella, who in turn was followed by Peter, struggling manfully to suppress the apprehensive look on his normally cheery face.

"I came after all, you see!" he declared to Miranda. "Mrs. Wordsworth-Pugh kindly asked me to act as escort to her party." He tried to look triumphant, but his gaze kept straying to where a string of bunting danced joyously in the wind. "You—you do not think we are in for a gale, do you?" he asked.

"A healthy breeze, nothing more," Miranda reassured him.

"A healthy breeze? How fortuitous!" exclaimed a voice from behind her.

Turning round Miranda found herself facing Arnold Denley who had also alighted from the Wordsworth-Pugh carriage.

"There, are you not astonished to see me, Miss Branscombe?" he beamed up at her. "I am taking your advice, you see. Lots of lovely fresh air, just as you suggested, and I am sure that already I am finding it beneficial."

"Cousin Denley is honouring us with yet another visit!" explained Peter, barely masking his tone of long suffering, then aside, through clenched teeth, he hissed at Miranda, "So it is you who is to blame for this second visitation, is it? He has done nothing but talk about the benefits of fresh air and exercise since he arrived.''

"I would have thought that any change in Mr. Denley's conversation was all to the good," Miranda whispered back.

"So I decided that sea air would be the thing," said Arnold Denley, who had apparently been carrying on a monologue quite unconcerned that no one was listening, "and where better than New Place, where the ozone is so bracing, and where my dear kinsfolk were so pressing in their invitation for me to pay a return visit?"

"That was Mother!" hissed Peter, again for Miranda's ears only. "The Old Gentleman refused to speak to her all morning as a consequence. Lor', it is bad enough having to go on a sea voyage without the added blessing of Cousin Denley!"

"You do not have to come," said Miranda.

"Oh but I do!" Denley thought she was addressing him. "Surely the air at sea must be the freshest in the world. Or does the salt taint it, do you think? Perhaps it would be unwise to inhale air that was tainted in any way. Think what salt does to bacon and herrings! No, perhaps you are right. I should not come."

"I am certain you have nothing to fear, for I am convinced that the air out at sea is of the purest and can only do you good," replied Miranda, ignoring Peter's frantic signals.

"Oh splendid! Then I shall come after all."

"Did you have to be so convincing?" mumbled Peter.

Miranda was saved from replying by Mrs. Wordsworth-Pugh's voice, piercing enough to cut through the work-a-day sounds of the busy shipyard.

"Why, there you are, my lord," she cried at full timbre. "We quite thought you had sailed away without us."

"A difficult feat, madam, seeing that the vessel is still firmly moored not five yards away," replied Oxenham, who had hoped to make a quiet entrance upon the group, so extracting the maximum effect by the unexpectedness of his appearance. His intentions had been marred by Mrs. Wordsworth-Pugh's eagle eyes.

His lordship was appalled at the size of the group awaiting him. Surely he had not invited all these people? Not young Kerswell, no never, nor that odd little dab of a cousin of his! Still, his mental faculties were not what they were; he was getting quite concerned about himself. Had he perhaps been foolish enough to add "and escorts" or "and friends" to the letters of invitation? It did not matter. Whatever he had written he refused to entertain such a crowd on board his vessel. This was a yacht bound for its sea-trials, not a packet-boat! They would all have to stay on shore! He opened his mouth to say so but was forestalled by Mrs. Wordsworth-Pugh.

"Ah, so that is your boat, my lord? And very splendid it is too. A most unusual figure-head, is it not, though I must say a little more drapery upon its upper anatomy might have been rather more proper.''

"It is artistic, Mama,'' interposed Miss Bella.

"Oh, artistic is it? In that case, no doubt, it will do very well. Come along, my darlings, let us get aboard. Richard, do hold Lucy's hand tightly lest she slip on the gangway.'' With these totally unnecessary instructions Mrs. Wordsworth-Pugh shepherded her party aboard, sweeping Peter along with her. Desperately he cast glances behind him, for his departure left Miranda alone on the dockside with Lord Oxenham.

"You were going to say something, my lord?'' she asked gently.

Oxenham closed his mouth. It was clearly open to no purpose now.

"It was not important,'' he said with a sigh.

"We should have a splendid day,'' said Miranda. "You were right, your yacht certainly does exceed all expectations. There is still one mystery, though—she does not have a name yet. Are you going to call her Nereid?''

"No,'' said Oxenham, who found he was suffering from an unaccountable brevity of conversation.

"Then may I ask what name you have chosen?''

Oxenham looked at his companion. She was lanky, plain and totally lacking in grace, yet when he was with her a strange feeling of contentment overcame him. Everything—or nearly everything—was right with the world when she was near him.

"Miranda,'' he said.

Miranda was startled.

"You would call such a beautiful vessel by my name?" she asked in astonishment.

Oxenham was equally startled. What on earth had possessed him to say that? Naming his yacht after her! But no, Miss Branscombe had made a nice distinction on that point. "Calling such a beautiful vessel by my name," she had said. How modest of her, and how sweet.

"Of course I would," Oxenham heard his own voice as if in a dream. "With your permission I should be delighted to call my yacht Miranda."

"So you have chosen a name at last, my lord!" Mr. Bray had arrived in time to overhear part of the conversation. "Miranda! What a pretty name, and so appropriate, for has it not some connection with the old stories of the sea, Greek or Latin or some such? Still, your lordship knows all about such things, no doubt, and that is why you chose it." Mr. Bray's sharp eyes were on Miss Branscombe's flushed cheeks, then he looked at Lord Oxenham's bemused expression and decided that if his lordship had named his yacht after some long-gone Greek nymph then Mrs. Bray's son was a Dutchman!

The little shipbuilder was at heart a romantic, but he was also a busy man with a ship to get to sea. He had been rather daunted by the large number of ladies and gentlemen who were to accompany the trip, but Miss Branscombe was among their number which was a relief. A quiet word in her ear and she was certain to keep them in order.

"Miss Branscombe, my lord, shall we go aboard now? Things are all ready for casting off." His pockets stuffed with notebooks, and his hands crammed with plans, he guided the last two passengers up the gangplank.

Peter had been watching this exchange from his vantage-point on deck, noting the change of expression on Miranda's face, and fuming at not being able to hear what was said. Every instinct urged him to rush back to the dockside and rescue Miranda from whatever it was that was bringing such colour to her cheeks, but he was hemmed in by Mrs. Wordsworth-Pugh, and escape from that lady in a determined mood was equal to escaping from the Château d'If.

The order to cast off came, and at once an organized flurry of activity swept over the elegant craft. The passengers were directed hither and thither in order to keep them out of the way of the crew and of the small bands of workmen who assiduously checked and rechecked every detail. Everything seemed to be going splendidly; only Miranda felt some unease, and the cause of her anxiety was Peter. She knew him so well, his frailties and his weakness, and she knew that a sea journey was the last thing he should have attempted. In the general frenzy of sailing she had not been able to keep as firm an eye on him as she would have wished. When she finally caught up with him he was deep in conversation with Miss Bella, or rather it was the young lady who was doing the talking. Peter was strangely silent and did not look at all happy.

"There is the most tempting-looking collation in the biggest room, or cabin I suppose I should call it. Mr. Denley and I had a peep in and it was truly sumptuous, I assure you. There were pastries, cold meat and lobsters—above all else I adore lobster, do you?"

The lady's recitation did not seem to be pleasing Peter. He looked quite strained. Miranda decided that rescue might be the order of the day.

"If I might borrow Mr. Kerswell from you for a moment, Miss Bella," she interposed, breaking into the recitation of gastronomic delights. "Peter, do tell me if that is old Mr. Fortescue waving to us from the headland. If it is he will be so put out if we do not return his greeting."

Gently she led him to a place of greater seclusion.

"Are you feeling poorly?" she asked kindly.

"Of course I am feeling poorly. You know I cannot set foot on any vessel without my entire inside going into revolt," Peter snapped back.

"Why do you not return to shore? The tug-boats have not yet cast off. You could go back with them."

"Do you mean we are not even under sail yet?" Horrified Peter stared over the side and found that a tiny flotilla of rowing-boats was still pulling them clear of the shore through a harbour that was as calm as a mill-pond.

"What, go ashore and leave you with—" he began, then shame and distress spread across his face.

"Oh dash it all, what shall I do? Not in front of Oxenham."

"If you will not go ashore then you must go below. I shall tell everyone you are examining the hull or something." Miranda neatly collared a passing crew member who understood the situation at a glance.

"Not too lively are we, sir?" he said. "You come along with me, I'll look after you, and we'll collect you a nice handy bucket on the way."

Peter's protest turned to groans as he was hurried below.

"Was that Mr. Kerswell?" asked Oxenham.

"It was. He has gone to explore below deck," replied Miranda innocently.

"Oh good." Oxenham was grateful for anything that relieved him of Peter's presence; then, in case he had sounded too amiable he added, "I only hope he will not rampage about the place and get in the way of Bray's people."

"I am certain he will do no such thing," replied Miranda with conviction.

"I am glad to hear it. Now tell me, do you like my yacht?" Why was her answer suddenly so important?

"I do indeed. At the dockside I thought she was the most beautiful thing I had seen, but here, truly afloat, she is more than beautiful, she is—is free! Does that sound foolish?"

"No, not at all. You describe her splendidly." Oxenham was struck by how exactly Miss Branscombe's feelings matched his own. That was just how he felt about sailing—the beauty and the freedom, and the knowledge that the whole world was within his grasp. He suddenly longed to take Miss Branscombe with him on a voyage. What a splendid companion she would be!

"You would love Greece," he said unexpectedly.

"Would I? Is that where you are going?"

"Perhaps. I am not certain, but it is a country that I am convinced would appeal to you. A magnificent land, still so primitive in parts and yet with the remains of one of the greatest civilizations everywhere about you."

"It sounds fascinating. I have long wished to see Greece." There was a gentle wistfulness in her voice. To travel to far lands was one of the dreams she scarcely dared to foster.

The longing in her voice touched Oxenham. He would beg her to come with him; surely it could be arranged. There had to be some way. Before he could give in to this crazy impulse Lord Oxenham found himself confronted by an extraordinary sight. He and Miranda had been slowly pacing the deck during their conversation, and their gentle ambling had brought them level with the foremast. There, seated comfortably on a barrel, his hat tethered to his head by a muffler, was Arnold Denley. He was securely lashed to the mast by a length of stout rope.

"Good heavens, what is this!" exclaimed Oxenham in astonishment. "Has the fellow had some premonition about foul weather or something?"

"I do hope it is all right, my lord, but the gentleman was most insistent," replied the bosun, who had been standing near by. "He kept on about fresh air and wanting a position where he would get most benefit. I hope I did the proper thing. I've never had such a request before, saving once when we hit dirty weather going round the Cape of Good Hope."

The seaman looked so anxious that Miranda smothered her chuckles in order to reassure him.

"The gentleman is just much concerned for his health," she said. "He looks perfectly happy, does he not? And he does not seem to be in the way there, so I dare say it is to everyone's advantage."

"You're right there, miss." The bosun beamed at her. "That gentleman had already caused a few near-mishaps by getting underfoot, and the captain were mortal affeared you ladies might hear some unbecoming language if something weren't done."

"I should leave the gentleman where he is and carry on with your own duties," ordered Oxenham. He was not sure whether or not he was sorry he had been so interrupted in his mad impulse to take Miranda to Greece. Upon reflection the whole scheme was too idiotic to contemplate seriously, yet now that the thread of his enthusiasm had been broken he was left with a curious sense of regret.

"Come, Miss Branscombe, let me show you my yacht properly," he said quickly, before any more madcap schemes could enter his head. "We are getting a fair breeze and the deck is a trifle unsteady, so, I beg of you, please take my arm.''

Miranda, whose sense of balance was excellent everywhere except upon the ballroom floor, accepted with pleasure. She found it very agreeable to be supported upon a gentleman's arm, for so often her very size daunted all but the most stout-hearted from ever offering such a service. They strolled about the deck as comfortably as the growing swell would permit, with Oxenham pointing out important features, particularly those of his own connivance. Miranda enjoyed it enormously; she found much to interest her and Oxenham was an attentive escort. It was only when Oxenham suggested that they should explore the quarters below deck that she had misgivings, not on account of her virtue, Miranda was too modest and honest ever to have regarded herself as an object of desire. Her concern was all for Peter, languishing somewhere in the bowels of the ship. She could not have him humiliated, particularly by the appearance of Oxenham. Peter's manly pride was saved by the arrival of the captain himself, a bluff individual with a wind-reddened face and the voice of a bull. Now, however, he controlled the volume to little more than a whisper.

''Your pardon, my lord,'' he said softly, ''but a matter of some delicacy has arisen, and I confess I am at a loss as to how to tackle it.''

"One of the ladies?" asked Oxenham, not pleased at having his conversation with Miranda interrupted yet again.

"Perhaps I should leave," said Miranda.

"Oh no, nothing like that. Indeed, miss, you might be able to think of something," said the captain hurriedly. "It concerns the gentleman who is at present lashed to the foremast. Something must be done about him and quickly. He keeps asking the crew if they know the form for burial at sea, and they are getting most upset." The captain's voice was growing in volume.

"Burial at sea?" Oxenham's face was a picture. "You mean he is planning to die on this trip? Can he not wait until we return to port?"

"What the gentleman's immediate plans are I have no idea, but his talk is upsetting my crew. We seamen are a superstitious lot, and if this ship should get a reputation for bad luck or something of the sort then we will have all manner of trouble."

"Indeed we will! Something must be done instantly!" agreed Oxenham.

Miranda considered for a moment. It was too much to expect Arnold Denley to cast off all his old ways completely.

"I think I can see someone who might be able to help," she said. "Mr. Griggs, we beg your assistance, if you please."

She beckoned to a middle-aged man with sharp blue eyes, one of Mr. Bray's people. Finding his services not needed for a few minutes he had been enjoying a quiet pipe. Now he came forward with a smile.

"Always ready to help you, Miss Branscombe, you know that. What do you want done?"

"A rather strange request, I am afraid. Mr. Griggs, you were a ship's carpenter before you worked for Mr. Bray, were you not?"

"That I was, miss. Fifteen years a chippy."

"And during that time you must have assisted at a number of burials at sea and be familiar with the ceremony. I believe that is part of a carpenter's duties?"

"That's right, miss, and I've done my share. Ah, would this have anything to do with the gentleman who is tied to the foremast? I gather he enjoys a bit of melancholy conversation."

"You understand perfectly," beamed Miranda. "Unfortunately few people have the qualifications or the inclination to satisfy him. Now, if you would be willing to engage him in conversation for a while and tell him some of your experiences we would be most obliged, but softly, if you please, so as not to distress the rest of the crew."

"Nothing easier, miss. I'll tell him about the time we got yellow fever off Louisiana. There should be enough melancholy in that tale to keep the gentleman happy."

"Mr. Griggs, you are a treasure. Come, I will introduce you to Mr. Denley. He will be delighted to make your acquaintance."

The carpenter followed Miranda forward, delight-edly pocketing the half-guinea slipped to him by a re-lieved Oxenham.

"Thank goodness that young lady was to hand, my lord," breathed the captain, wiping his brow. "Understood the problem in a flash, did she not? And came up with just the right solution. Could have been a very tricky situation, but she put it all to rights. A most exceptional young lady, yes most exceptional!"

Lord Oxenham entertained similar views about Miranda Branscombe. She had a positive talent for smoothing away troubles. Why, on this short voyage alone she had averted several minor mishaps; he had noticed her gently but firmly shepherding the other ladies to resting-places where they would not trip up the crew; and she certainly knew how to handle that Denley fellow without seeming to be in the least man-aging. Without her this trip would have been fraught with disasters.

At this point the darker side of Lord Oxenham's intellect pointed out that without Miranda Bran-scombe there would have been none of the problems in the first place, for it was only in an attempt to please her that he had burdened himself with such a ram-shackle set of people.

There was no denying the truth of this observation, but then if he had not had Miranda Branscombe as his companion on this sea-trip who would he have cho-sen? Maria Whitelea? Kitty Alphington? Why, they would have shrieked and squawked all over the ship, teased the workmen, and lured the more virile members of the crew down into the cabins below deck. No, the very thought made Oxenham shudder and close his eyes. When he opened them again it was with the clear conviction that he was pleased to have Miranda with him, no matter how odd some of her friends, and that there was no other woman he would sooner have for company. For a man who had formerly regarded his female acquaintances by the dozen this was a breathtaking observation, so much so that for a full quarter of an hour his lordship was quite unable to attend to the conversation of the captain.

Miranda had no idea that she was having such a shattering effect upon his lordship. Just at present her attention was directed upon seeing that Mr. Denley enjoyed a splendidly funereal conversation with Mr. Griggs, so that he caused no more trouble.

"Miss Branscombe, I might have known that you would find for me the most interesting fellow," Mr. Denley cried in delight.

"Mr. Griggs will give you all the information you seek," said Miranda. "But before I leave you, are you sure that you are comfortable?"

"Splendidly thank you." Denley wiggled his bonds. "One of those kind sailors found me a barrel to sit upon, and he assured me that here I would enjoy the purest and freshest air on the whole trip, and I am convinced that he is right."

"Then if you will excuse me I will leave you to enjoy your chat with Mr. Griggs." Miranda hurried away down the nearby companion-way. She was going in search of Peter, and her conscience smote her because she had neglected him for so long. She only hoped that his sufferings had not been too great. Her hopes were in vain. She easily found Peter merely by following the sound of his groans.

"Hullo, miss." The sailor, Peter's ministering angel, grinned at her through tobacco-stained teeth. "Come to see the young gentleman, have you? My, he's a rare one. Not seen anything like it, not in twenty-odd years of sea-faring. I keep telling him it'll make a new man of him, for 'struth, there can't be much of the old one left."

"I will kill that man, if only I live!" groaned Peter, whose sense of humour had long since gone over the side.

"Oh, poor dear. Is there anything you want?" murmured Miranda.

"Only to die, but not before I have got my hands round that rogue's scrawny neck!"

"There, didn't I say he was a rare one?" chuckled the sailor.

"I am sure you must have other duties awaiting you," said Miranda, who was beginning to suspect a lack of sympathy between patient and nurse. "I will stay with the gentleman now."

"Thank you, miss. I must say I could do with finding myself a few vittles—a nice bit of fat bacon, maybe, or a rich mutton pie with plenty of gravy."

Miranda did not see him go, she was too busy attending to an anguished Peter, but she heard the sailor chuckling to himself as he hurried on deck.

"A devil incarnate, that is what he was," moaned Peter, when he had regained his composure. "I swear Oxenham only took him on to torment me."

"Never mind, he has gone now. I have begged a lemon from the cook, and some dry biscuits."

"That is food!" cried Peter. "Why do you bring me food? Even that devil only tormented me with the thought of it, you have brought it within distance of my nostrils."

"Try nibbling the biscuit slowly," said Miranda, ignoring his tirade. "And if you feel that that is beyond you then suck a little of the lemon. You will feel better by and by."

"I shall never feel better," said Peter resolutely. "All of my sympathies go out to my Cousin Denley. I have gravely wronged that man. I now know how it feels to face impending death."

"You would do better to face an impending biscuit. Besides, your Cousin Denley is in robust health at this moment, lashed to the foremast and listening to a tale of death and disease off the Louisiana coast, in company with Miss Bella. I never saw him in stouter form."

"You did not tell anyone where I was, did you?" asked Peter, obediently nibbling on a biscuit.

"Of course not. Besides, I did not know myself until I heard you groaning. Just lift your head, will you, while I put this pillow under you. You will feel less giddy propped up a little.''

Peter looked shame-faced.

''I am making a proper cake of myself am I not? Everyone else is perfectly happy on this sea-trip, even poor little Denley. Only I have to succumb like a hysterical girl. I, who was going to protect you from Oxenham, and here you are, looking after me. You must think me an absolute ninny-hammer.''

''No, I do not,'' said Miranda firmly. ''I know how you hate being at sea, and how ill it makes you, yet you insisted upon coming for my sake. I think that was very brave of you. Wrong-headed, for I was not in the least danger, you know, but sweet and brave just the same.''

''Good old Miranda, always thinking the best of the most hopeless cases. I do not know how you do it.''

''I do it because it is true. Now, I will cover you with this rug, and you are to close your eyes and go to sleep.''

''No, I flatly refuse to sleep! I may not be much of a success at defending you so far but while you are by my side I can at least stay vigilant. Who knows. Oxenham might come down to see where you are.''

''I doubt it very much. He was with the captain when I left, and doubtless they have a lot to discuss about the yacht. She seems to be sailing very sweetly, though I doubt if you will agree with me. Still, you need not worry for much longer, we are on the homeward run and your misery will soon be over. That will please you, will it not?''

But Miranda received no answer, for Peter Kerswell, defender of maidens' honour and her self-appointed protector had fallen fast asleep. Miranda smiled gently to herself, removed the half-eaten biscuit from his hand and tiptoed away.

CHAPTER NINE

LORD OXENHAM paced his cramped quarters at the inn with the restlessness of a caged lion, feeling quite unable to account for the unsettled state of his emotions. Yesterday the sea-trials of his yacht had proved exceedingly satisfactory, modifications to the craft would be negligible and Mr. Bray was confident that she would be ready well ahead of the promised date. There was nothing, therefore, to keep his lordship in the district, the local society was scarcely amusing, his accommodation fell short of tolerable. Why, then, was he finding it so difficult to tell Mallard to pack his bags and order the carriage?

Could it be that a poetic mood was about to engulf him? Oxenham considered the idea seriously—and discounted it. He had not written anything worthwhile in ages, not since he had realized that his adoring public would have swooned over any words written by his hand, whether they be the outpourings of his soul or his laundry-list. No, his poetic muse had deserted him, along with his taste for scandalous living and for women like Maria Whitelea. Maria Whitelea! Oxenham allowed his mind to dwell upon her for a moment, and upon as many of her predecessors as his memory could cope with. He did not even bother to suppress the shudder the recollection caused. When there were women like Miranda Branscombe in this world why on earth had he expended so much of his youthful energies upon the Maria Whiteleas? It was then that he found the solution to his restlessness! He would call upon Miss Branscombe immediately. There was something very important he wanted to say to her!

It was as well that his lordship was a little tardy in coming to this conclusion, otherwise he would have found Miranda already engaged.

Miranda had spent the morning very pleasantly resuming her domestic duties. However, she was concerned about Peter. He had looked so white and exhausted when the voyage had ended, and it had taken all her ingenuity to smuggle him ashore secretly without the other members of the party seeing his distressed state. Even now she was not convinced that Mrs. Wordsworth-Pugh believed her story about him still assisting Mr. Bray counting the number of planks in the hull, but it was the best she could conjure under difficult circumstances. Now she was sitting at her writing-desk, penning a short note to New Place, enquiring how Peter fared after a night on *terra firma*. She was just finishing when Mr. Denley was announced.

"Why, Mr. Denley, what a pleasant surprise! How well you are looking," she said.

"And may I be permitted to say that you are in splendid looks yourself?" replied Denley.

"That is very kind of you." Miranda looked at him curiously. There was something different about him this morning, a certain assertiveness in his manner that she had not seen before.

Unknown to Miranda the previous day had proved a watershed in the hypochondria-bound life of Arnold Denley. Having been parted from all medical assistance for a whole day by a mile or so of sea he had been astounded to find that he had not minded! Lashed to his vantage-point in the freshest of fresh air, listening to Mr. Grigg's gloomy discourse and Miss Bella's more cheery chatter, he had been so diverted that he had completely forgotten about his health for minutes at a time. Finally, after the trip was over and he should have been half-dead with fatigue he had found his services urgently in demand. Mrs. Wordsworth-Pugh and her daughters were in need of a sensible gentleman escort, Mr. Kerswell being curiously absent and Mr. Branscombe made even more curiously idiotic by love. All the responsibility for seeing the party safely home had fallen upon Denley, and strangely enough he had enjoyed it. It was a new experience for him to be protective and in command. He had even been bold enough to call out, "Here, fellow, go more slowly. You are frightening the ladies," to the coachman.

This new-found confidence had lasted right through the night, instilling an unusual determination within Denley's meagre breast. For some time he had been toying with vague thoughts of matrimony. Today seemed a good opportunity to act. Arnold Denley had come to propose! He did consider throwing himself on his knees before the lady, this being the required posture, seemingly, but not wishing to suffer the agonies of rheumatism he elected to remain standing. This did at least give him a unique opportunity to be able to look down upon the lady in question. Alas, Denley's researches into the technique of proposing had been sketchy, and his knowledge of the appropriate language was even less.

"Miss Branscombe," he began, "it is several years since my dear Mama left me for a Higher Sphere, and I miss her sorely. I am sadly bereft of anyone to care for me or to tend me with proper sympathy in my hour of suffering— I discount my servants, the lower orders have no instinct for proper sympathy. So, until I am fortunate enough to join Mama in her Heavenly Pastures I think I must have a wife. I flatter myself that I have much to offer a suitable lady, unlimited opportunities for one with true compassion. I notice that most members of your sex are at their happiest when they are caring for someone, and you, my dear Miss Branscombe, have the greatest talent I have ever encountered for bringing relief to the sick and suffering. Think what pleasure life as my spouse could afford you, supervising my diet, ensuring that I take just the right amount of healthy exercise, sitting, watchful and tender, by my bedside should I suffer a relapse. Think how delightful it will be! Please say yes, I beg of you, for already you have brought relief to a chronic invalid such as myself. I am convinced that you are the helpmate for my few remaining years." Denley warmed to his subject. If one could not enjoy the benefits of delicious ill health oneself then surely the next best thing must be to tend one who did? True, he was in robust form at the moment but it was not a state of affairs he intended to continue, so it was only fair to show Miss Branscombe what a delightful time would be in store for her as Mrs. Denley. Belatedly, more mundane inducements occurred to him and he added, "Besides which, Miss Branscombe, I am not a poor man. Oh dear me no! I have ten thousand a year clear, a fine house in Somerset positioned on rising ground and with most excellent drains, and my Town house is most advantageously situated on the route to Highgate Cemetery."

He looked at Miranda expectantly, waiting for her to speak.

Miranda was blessed with a strong sense of humour, and the mode of this proposal, so far removed from even her most unromantic dreams, might have sent her into uncontrolled laughter had not the kindness of her heart been even greater. After all, this was her first proposal, something she had never expected to receive, and she was both grateful and touched.

"Mr. Denley, this is a great honour you have done me," she began, confident that so far at least she was on safe ground. "In fact, it is the greatest honour a gentleman can bestow upon a lady. I am truly sorry for your plight, you must be very lonely and uncomfortable at times, and I agree whole-heartedly that you should have a wife to care for you, but regrettably I do not think that I am the right person for that very important position. This is too serious a matter for anything but complete honesty, so I must confess that while I like you my affections are not sufficiently engaged to consider matrimony, for without such affections I am certain I could never make you happy. I hope you are not disappointed for I am sure you will soon find someone who will bring you all the happiness you deserve." Miranda felt she had acquitted herself satisfactorily for someone unused to rejecting suitors, for she really did not want to hurt the little man's feelings.

Denley, however, was not at all hurt, merely curious.

"Does this mean you do not want to look after me?" he asked in some astonishment.

"If you are ill and truly need someone, then I would gladly come and nurse you," said Miranda gently. "But the qualities you require in a nurse are very different from those you would wish for in a wife. A competent nurse can always be hired, you know. There are several of my acquaintance that I would be glad to recommend. A wife, however, is quite a different matter."

"I had not thought of that," confessed Mr. Denley, who was still a little sorry for Miss Branscombe, throwing away such a wonderful opportunity. "But you do not think you might reconsider your decision at some later date?'' Miranda's shake of the head was sympathetic but very definite. ''Ah well, then there is no more to be said except to wish you a cordial farewell, Miss Branscombe.''

Mr. Denley left Branscombe Hall deep in thought. Miss Branscombe was a lady whose opinions he genuinely valued, and since she would not marry him the least he could do was follow her advice. He would look for a wife elsewhere, but where? Miss Bella Wordsworth-Pugh came into his mind. Capable and intelligent, she had the added bonus of being exceedingly pretty. As his footsteps veered towards the new object of his attentions Denley mentally reviewed his manner of proposing—after all, he was now a man of some experience in such matters. Some latent instinct warned him that this time, so as to avoid being rejected a second time, it might be better if he began with his houses and his ten thousand a year clear.

Back at Branscombe Hall an anguished cry rang through the house, causing the servants to pause in their tasks. Sir Henry had just been informed by his daughter that she had actually refused a proposal of marriage.

''What folly!'' he cried. ''Miranda, have you taken leave of your senses? To refuse after all the trouble we have taken to find you a husband! You should have consulted me, it was the least you could have done!''

''Perhaps I should, Papa. I am sorry, but I am convinced the marriage would not have been a success. A match where the only affinity is a working knowledge of the medicine-chest cannot be said to have a firm foundation, can it? Besides, would you really like me to go away and live in Somerset? It would leave you all alone to cope with Mrs. Wordsworth-Pugh.''

The truth of this observation struck Sir Henry forcibly as did a vision of Mrs. Wordsworth-Pugh advancing purposefully down the aisle towards him, those frightful plumes quivering in a predatory manner. It was horrifying enough to make him temporarily forget his eagerness to get Miranda married.

''Perhaps you are right, my dear,'' he said. ''Somerset is a most inconvenient distance. And after all, you have received an offer, have you not? That is something, even if it did not suit—and having received one what is to say that you might not get another, eh? But if not, then you can stay at home and look after your poor old papa.''

Miranda smiled, for Sir Henry was looking anything but poor and old. In fact he was looking exceedingly handsome and elegant in his russet velvet cut-away coat and dove-grey pantaloons.

''I would like that, even though I know my prime function would be to protect my Papa from all those ladies who find him irresistible.''

''Stuff and nonsense! Run along now, there is a good girl!'' beamed Sir Henry, delighted by her remark.

After the door had closed behind her, however, his face grew thoughtful. There were factors in the matter of Miranda's marriage which had not occurred to him before. She really was the most useful creature to have about the place; he had quite forgotten what it was to have trouble with the servants or quarrelsome tenants since she had been old enough to take charge. How would he manage without her? But most of all how would he keep Mrs. Wordsworth-Pugh at bay all by himself? In the coming years he was bound to be in that lady's company a great deal once her daughter was married to Richard, and supposing, as he grew older and his resistance lessened, he dropped his guard just once, it would be exactly the opportunity that the lady sought. She would have him in front of the vicar before you could say knife and he would be condemned to a dotage filled with puce plumes. It was more than he could bear. No, Miranda would have to remain single, she was his last line of defence. And yet it was such a disgrace to have an unmarried daughter, particularly one who still showed every indication of becoming a second Great-Aunt Evangeline. Was ever a man so beset with difficulties? It was then that Sir Henry recollected someone else. Mrs. Bakewell, the pretty little widow whose company he had often sought of late. She was a charming companion, elegant and musical, and above all devoid of plumes. Might she not provide him with a very acceptable means of escape if the worst came to the worst? Sir Henry gave a sigh of relief and lay back against the sofa cushions quite worn out by the anguish of the last five minutes. Miranda or Emma Bakewell, either way he would not be left to face Mrs. Wordsworth-Pugh alone and unprotected.

Quite unaware of the agony she had so recently provoked in her father Miranda settled down to the household accounts, but before long she was interrupted by the butler.

"Lord Oxenham has called to see you, Miss Miranda," he announced. "I have put him in the Yellow Drawing-room."

"Thank you, Banks. I expect his lordship is due to leave the district and has come to say his farewells."

"Miss Branscombe, how well you are looking," Oxenham greeted her as she entered the room.

This was true, for the experience of receiving a proposal of marriage was a flattering one and had brought a flush to Miranda's cheeks and a sparkle to her eyes, so that, if not pretty, she was at least looking her best.

"Thank you, my lord. I fancy the air at Branscombe suits me better than that of London."

There followed a silence while Miranda waited for her guest to make some formal remark about his regret at quitting the district, prior to saying his farewell. No such remark came. Lord Oxenham seemed strangely ill at ease, refusing her offers of either a chair or refreshment. The silence threatened to become embarrassing; then Lord Oxenham suddenly blurted out, "Miss Branscombe, I have something to say to you. A favour, I suppose in a way. This is devilish awkward. I know not where to begin."

Miranda, witnessing his evident distress, yearned to help him and racked her brains for the possible cause of his discomfort.

"I think I know what troubles you!" she cried at last, as his lordship grew more and more tongue-tied. "And of course I understand, and do not mind one bit. You must do as you think fit, for I know the matter is close to your heart."

"I beg your pardon?" Oxenham was bewildered by this incomprehensible answer to a question he had not yet asked.

"Your yacht. You have changed your mind about the name and would prefer something other than Miranda. That is what you have come about, is it not?"

"Good heavens no!" exclaimed his lordship. "I came to ask you to marry me."

The silence which fell upon the Yellow Drawing-room exceeded anything that chamber had experienced in a long and varied history.

"Marriage?" said Miranda in a very small voice.

"Oh what a fool you must think me! To have blurted it out in such a fashion!" Lord Oxenham groaned aloud and clapped both hands to his head in a gesture of anguish. "Your pardon, Miss Branscombe. I had intended to approach the subject in a very different manner. My inexperience in proposing matrimony must be my only excuse. I had thought myself to be a lifelong bachelor, so it is a matter I have always regarded with the utmost wariness. Would you like me to start again?"

"I should not like to put you to such bother, my lord," replied Miranda weakly. She scarcely knew which bemused her the most, the purpose of Lord Oxenham's visit, the abrupt manner of his delivery, or his serious suggestion that he should repeat the whole process. Struggling hard to retrieve a rapidly departing composure she went on, "There is no need for a repetition, my lord, for you were exceedingly clear and easy to understand. I thank you for not prevaricating. It is extremely discommoding not knowing exactly what is being asked of one."

"You have had other recent proposals?" asked Lord Oxenham suspiciously. This was a deuced inconvenient moment to learn of a possible rival.

"One, my lord." Try as she might Miranda could not suppress a small thrill of satisfaction at being able to utter those words honestly.

"And might I ask what your answer was? I have no wish to importune you further if you are promised to another."

"I declined the honour, my lord."

"Would—would it be improper of me to ask why? Seeing as I have a vested interest, as it were."

"Not at all, my lord. I felt that I did not have enough affection for the gentleman to make him a good wife."

Lord Oxenham found himself swallowing hard. Used as he was to being at ease in all situations, he was discovering that this proposing business was much more complicated than he had anticipated. He considered Miranda's last statement, then all at once he relaxed, convinced he was doing the right thing. She really was the dearest girl.

"If I may say so, Miss Branscombe, that was a typical remark," he said, smiling gently. "Any other lady would have said, 'I did not have enough affection to be happy with him.'"

"It is merely the way I saw the situation," replied Miranda.

"I know, and if, at this very moment, I were suffering any doubts about the course of action I am taking then that one sentence of yours would have assured me it was the most sensible thing I have ever done. You would have to have affection for your husband?"

"Affection or a very deep respect, my lord."

"Miss Branscombe, I know I blurted out my original request in a most churlish way, but it was sincere, I promise you. Have you recovered from the shock sufficiently to give the matter serious consideration?"

"I have been doing so since the moment you spoke," replied Miranda honestly.

"And might I hope for some sort of answer? I have known many ladies—to hide that fact from you would be pointless—alas, my reputation precedes me wherever I go. Some of it, to my shame is deserved, but much is sorely exaggerated. I tell you this because never before have I met any lady who made the state of matrimony even slightly tempting, not until I met you. When I am with you I feel so comfortable and pleased with life. You are so—so good for me. I would be worthy of you, dearest Miss Branscombe, I would indeed.''

Miranda looked at the earnest expression on his handsome face. What was she to reply to this astonishing proposal that had come to her as unexpectedly as any thunderbolt from the heavens? This was a far harder decision than turning down Arnold Denley, but one which required just as much honesty.

''My lord,'' she said, carefully considering every word before she spoke, ''I fear you will think me very missish when I say that your proposal has taken me completely by surprise. I have enjoyed your company exceedingly this summer, but never did I expect it to lead to matrimony. Indeed, I have never even considered marriage for myself, for I know perfectly well my own limitations. No man wants a very plain wife unless she brings an enormous dowry to compensate him, and you, my lord, could choose from so many. I know that I like you very much. Nay, I will go further and say that I have a great fondness for you, but before I commit us both to a life of matrimony I must beg a little time to consider. I do not think that my favourable opinion of you is because I am flattered by your attentions, but I would prefer to be absolutely sure. Marriage should be a happy state, and sooner than bring you anything less I would prefer to remain an old maid.''

Lord Oxenham attended to her reply carefully and found that he was more delighted with it than if she had given an outright acceptance. Miranda Branscombe's answer would be nothing less than totally honest.

"Of course you shall have time to consider, Miss Branscombe. I know I have caught you unawares. You have not refused me out of hand and that pleases me. May I in turn ask one more favour? Might I ask your father for permission to pay my addresses formally? That way, if he accepts me as your acknowledged suitor, we will have the chance to be in each other's company all the more, and so give you a greater opportunity to make up your mind. If, upon closer acquaintance, you find that you could not share your life with me then you would be perfectly free to say so.''

"That is a most generous and sensible suggestion, my lord. It would please me to see you more often, but only if you too feel free to withdraw your offer if you have second thoughts. I promise I will not cry the jilted maid,'' Miranda smiled.

"There is scant fear of that, Miss Branscombe. Might I speak to Sir Henry now, do you think? Is he free?''

"I am sure that he is. I will not accompany you, though, if you will excuse me. It will be better if you speak to him alone.''

Miranda watched as the door closed behind this, her second and even more unexpected suitor, and felt thankful to be alone with her agitated thoughts. Oxenham was a delightful friend and so very handsome, he would be a marvellous match. Yet there was so much to consider carefully. Could she tolerate his probable unfaithfulness—for he was too attractive a dog to learn the trick of fidelity now? But even more, did she care enough about him to take the enormous step of matrimony?

Yes, Miranda had a great deal to think about.

CHAPTER TEN

WHEN PETER ARRIVED at Branscombe Hall next day he found the place humming with suppressed excitement. Although Miranda had begged Sir Henry to be discreet about the change in her relationship with Lord Oxenham, somehow the news had leaked out. Filtering through the domestics, it had gained momentum on its journey downwards through the social orders, so that while Banks, the butler, rejoiced in Miss Miranda's possible marriage, little Meg, the tweeny, wept salt tears into the washing-up water because she thought her beloved mistress was to be wed at any minute and would be going away.

Peter walked into this turmoil unawares, but Richard soon enlightened him.

"What do you think? Deuced good news. Miranda has had an offer!" he declared.

"No!" Peter stood stock-still, then a beam of delight spread across a face still pale from his nautical adventures. "Do not tell me that Cousin Denley has turned up trumps? That is capital! It will make Miranda my cousin, too, now, will it not? Splendid! Absolutely splendid!"

"No, no, not Denley!" Richard could not imagine how his friend could be so stupid. "It was Oxenham who offered. She has not given a definite reply yet, but I am convinced she will accept him. She would be a fool not to do so. Papa is quite beside himself with delight. He had to go and have a lie down on the library sofa."

"Oxenham?" The smile faded from Peter's face, leaving it even more ashen than before. "Oxenham? You cannot be serious!"

"Incredible, eh?" The news had been startling enough to penetrate even Richard's love-besotted state. "But seemingly Oxenham has taken a fancy to her, so there you are! A marvellous match, is it not?"

"No, it is not!" said Peter flatly. "You are out of your mind, and so is Sir Henry, for even considering it."

"Oh, here, I say! Steady on, old fellow! Say what you like about me by all means, but have a care how you speak about Papa. To say he is out of his mind ain't respectful."

"My apologies." Peter curbed his tongue with an effort. "Let me put it another way. Surely your father does not consider Lord Oxenham to be a fit and proper husband for Miranda?"

"Why ever not? Now it is you who is out of his mind. Oxenham is rich and has a title, as well as being a good-looking fellow. The coat he was wearing this morning was as fine a bit of tailoring as I have seen.

Excellent grey broadcloth, single-breasted with a high collar—"

"The devil take his coat and his high collar!" roared Peter. "This is Miranda's future we are discussing—"

"And discussing it very loudly," interposed Miranda, coming into the room. "You can be heard all over the house. I gather you have learnt of the great honour Lord Oxenham has done me. I suppose it is too late to ask that the matter is not spread throughout the country, but I beg you to do your best."

"The honour! Oxenham did you no honour. An offer of marriage coming from such a libertine is nothing less than an insult to a respectable female," declared Peter, lowering his voice.

"Oh dear, that is a very familiar tune," sighed Miranda.

"And will continue to be familiar until I get you to realize the folly of considering such a notion. There is not a sin or a vice that Oxenham has not dabbled in. His reputation is known from Cornwall to Cumberland, and yet you are thinking of marrying him."

"Indeed I am. I like him very much."

"You like everyone, even old Tam, the tinker, who has never washed in his life and smells worse than a herd of goats, so that is no recommendation. Think again, Miranda, this man is wicked and cold-hearted. He cares naught for the feelings of others, least of all women, though no doubt he has sworn to you that he will turn over a new leaf. Ah, I see by your face that I am right. Surely you were not taken in by such non-sense?''

"I believe in the honesty of his intentions, even if I do not expect him to maintain them for very long. Life as Lady Oxenham would not be easy. I realize that, but I do not think it would be unpleasant or distasteful. I am very fond of him, otherwise I would not have considered his offer for a moment. That would be most unfair to Lord Oxenham.''

"Oh, you have not been taken in by his romantic image, have you?'' cried Peter in disgust. "The one that all the stupid females swoon over? No, not you, the most sensible girl I know? You would never be such a fool!''

"I am fond of him,'' repeated Miranda. "More than that is not your concern, dear friend though you are.''

"But it is my concern. I would be a poor friend indeed if I let you go through with it.''

"You can do nothing to stop it. Papa has given his approval, even though it is too early for such things. He is absolutely delighted.''

"But you cannot marry Oxenham just to please your father, especially when he does not seem to appreciate the character of the man.''

"But I think it is a very good reason. I have always been such a disappointment to him it would make up for everything. Everything. Besides, I think I would enjoy being Lady Oxenham.''

"Do you want a title so much?''

"You know better than that."

"Yes, you are right. I am sorry. Such a thought would never have occurred to you. Oh, Miranda, you are far too good to be thrown away on a man like Oxenham. There must be something I can do. I am determined to prevent the match. Sooner than let you marry Oxenham I would—I would—dash it all, Miranda, I would marry you myself! Now why did I not think of it before? It is the perfect solution. Of course I will only be a baronet when my Old Gentleman goes to his just reward, but I dare say you will not mind that, and my fortune will be a very tidy one. Added to which you will only have to step across the park to reach your new home, which should certainly please your father. Perhaps he will not object to me as a son-in-law, and I know Mama and my Old Gentleman would be delighted to have you in our family, they both are exceedingly fond of you. Yes, it is the obvious solution. I had best go and have a word with Sir Henry at once. I may need to persuade him a little if I am to marry you, but he will get used to the idea by and by. Is he still in the library, do you know?" Peter was making purposefully for the door when Miranda's voice made him stop.

"No!" she said.

"No?" Peter turned. "Then if Sir Henry is not in the library no doubt Banks will know where he is. Ring the bell, if you please, Richard, there's a good fellow."

"No—no—no—no!" repeated Miranda, her voice shaking. "I mean no, I will not marry you! I do not know why you ever supposed that I would."

Peter froze. "Not marry me? I do not understand."

"You do not?" Miranda's face had gone red and her eyes were strangely bright. "It is all very easy, if you concentrate. There is no need for you to disturb Papa or Banks or anyone else because I am not going to marry you. I suppose I should be grateful for the offer but I am not! I would sooner marry Oxenham—or—or Denley, or—or—or even Tam the tinker! In fact, I would not marry you if you were the last man in the world!" So saying, she gave a great sob and rushed from the room, leaving both young men staring at each other as if the end of the world had come.

"Oh, I say, here is a to-do!" said Richard, his own cheeks pink with distress.

"She does not want to marry me! Miranda does not want to marry me!" In spite of the simplicity of Miranda's statement, and the clarity of her delivery Peter was still having trouble comprehending her message.

"She was crying," whispered Richard in awe.

Peter did not reply. He simply stood there transfixed by bewilderment and disbelief.

"She does not want to marry me!" he said again.

"She was crying," repeated Richard.

"Eh?" Richard's words filtered into Peter's stunned brain.

"I said, Miranda was crying when she left—and Miranda never cries. Oh, what possessed you to make such a crackbrained suggestion? Now she is all upset!" Richard wrung his hands.

"She cannot be crying."

"But she was, and it is all your fault."

"But I do not understand. I only suggested— She was crying, you say? And she will not marry me. Why will she not marry me? Oh, I have made her cry! What shall I do? Miranda! Miranda!" It was a thoroughly distressed and confused Peter who rushed from the room, leaving Richard blowing his nose vigorously.

In his headlong flight Peter cannoned into Nanny Hart, once dictator of the Branscombe nursery and now doyenne of the domestic staff.

"My, whatever is amiss, Mr. Peter?" she demanded when he set her on her feet again.

"I have done something awful, Nanny, the worst thing I have ever done in my life. I have made Miss Miranda cry!" Peter's voice was still that of a stunned man.

The old servant pulled herself up to her full height, diminutive though that was.

"And just what have you been saying to my Miss Miranda to upset her?" she demanded, glaring at him full in the waistcoat buttons.

"That is what is so bewildering. I only said that I would marry her sooner than let her go to Lord Oxenham. That was all."

"That was all, was it?" The scorn in Nanny's voice was terrible. "Well, it was more than enough, seemingly. It never fails to amaze me how stupid some clever young gentlemen can be!"

Peter did not understand her words, but he was too upset to bother.

"She would not have me, Nanny! Not if I was the last man in the world, she said! What have I done to make her dislike me so? I must see her! I must talk to her!" He made to go upstairs, but Nanny Hart blocked his way.

"You will stay here *if* you please, Master Peter!" she commanded, using a mode of address and tone of voice she had not employed on him for a good fifteen years. "Going up to a young lady's room! I have never heard of such a thing! I will enquire if my Miss wishes to speak with you."

Peter sank down on the stairs to await her return, his head clasped in his hands, a picture of utter despair. It was there that Banks found him, and the butler was so alarmed at seeing the usually ebullient Mr. Kerswell so distraught that he fetched him a large glass of brandy at once.

"Drink this and you will soon feel better, sir," he said, pressing the glass into Peter's limp hand.

"I will never feel better. I made Miss Miranda cry," replied Peter. It did not matter how often he repeated that statement the full horror of it failed to diminish.

"Did you, sir? Well, I am sure Miss Miranda will soon forgive you."

"But I will never forgive myself! Not ever! Not if I live to be as old as Methuselah. Have you ever known Miss Miranda to cry, Banks?"

"I must admit that I cannot quite recall such an event, sir." The butler was at a loss as to how to cope with this crisis. Normally, in such a situation, he would have called Miss Miranda, but under the circumstances that did not seem a very appropriate course of action. Instead he replenished the glass of brandy, the first having been demolished in one gulp, and then made his excuses to withdraw. Peter sat on. His whole world had lurched from beneath him, and even now it continued to shake, and the awful thing was that he did not know how or why.

"Miss Miranda will see you in her sitting-room now," said Nanny Hart from the top of the stairs. "Ten minutes only, mind. I shall be right outside the door, so see you behave yourself, Mr. Peter, or I will come in and box your ears, big as you are!"

Miranda was standing with her back to him when he entered, blowing her nose. She did not turn to face him, so he just stood there, not knowing what to say. He felt awkward in her presence, one more new and terrible experience in a day which was rapidly developing into the worst he had ever spent. He had never ever felt awkward with Miranda before, not even when she had held his head during the distressing aftermath of his first indulgence in a whole bottle of wine, or when she had dried his youthful tears after an interview with his Old Gentleman had made it too painful to sit down. She had always been dear old Miranda, a comfort and a refuge to both him and Richard, yet now she stood aloof and hostile like a stranger.

"Well, you wished to speak to me. Why do you not say something?" demanded Miranda at length. She even sounded different, almost waspish.

"I have come to say that I am sorry." The words fell limp and inadequate upon his own ears.

"You have, have you? Your apology is accepted, though I have no notion why you should feel the need to apologize." Again there was that unfamiliar sharpness of tone.

"I made you cry."

"Do not flatter yourself, Peter Kerswell. I have had a very—very emotional time recently, that is all. Things got a little too much for me."

Peter hung his head. He did not believe her, but he could think of no reply.

"Have you finished or do you wish to torment me further? I know that I am looking even more frightful than usual and that I have made a complete fool of myself. Is that not sufficient for one day? Have I not entertained you enough?"

"Oh Miranda!" cried Peter, hurt that she should accuse him of such a thing.

"'Oh Miranda!' Is that all you can say?"

"No, why would you marry Oxenham but not me?" This had bewildered him, he could not understand it. Ever since childhood he and Richard had been able to count upon Miranda's unwavering adoration. It had cherished them both all through their schooldays, through pimply adolescence and into manhood. Richard still had that adoration—he was, after all, her brother—but Peter had been cast out! The world had suddenly become a very cold and unbearable place. He felt totally bereft. Miranda preferred someone else to him. "Why would you marry Oxenham but not me?" he repeated.

"I cannot marry you both, 'tis against the law of the land."

"Oh, give me a proper answer, it is unlike you to give such tart replies! You said you would not consider me as a husband and I must know why."

"For one thing Oxenham asked me first, though to be truthful, I do not recall you asking me at all. Apparently you were so confident of my reply you considered it quite unnecessary to consult me."

"And you are piqued, is that it?" So simple an answer had not occurred to him. He began to feel better. "If I had come to you with a bunch of red roses in one hand and a sonnet in the other you would have had me, is that it?"

"But you did not, did you?" The coldness of Miranda's tone caused his brief burst of confidence to wither and perish. "And do not inflict me with a revised version of your proposal, I pray you, for it will not wash. I do not know why you are making so much fuss about Lord Oxenham. You and Richard have tried for ages to find me a husband, and now I have got one, or a prospective one at least. Indeed, if it had

not been for your efforts I would never have met Oxenham in the first place.''

Peter gave a groan at learning that he had been the
author of his own misery.

"Or perhaps you are annoyed because I would not
have your Cousin Denley," continued Miranda.

"That is a preposterous idea," Peter retorted.
"There is a world of difference between my cousin and
that libertine."

"Not so much. They both want to wed someone
who will make them comfortable. Your Cousin Denley wants someone who will persuade him that he is
not ill, and Oxenham wants someone who will persuade him that he is not bored. Why should you object because I choose one and not the other?"

Yes, why did he object? He had been able to regard
Miranda's possible marriage to Denley with perfect
equanimity, so why was he now so distressed at the
thought of her becoming Oxenham's wife? It was
more than just the man's bad character, Peter was
honest enough to realize that. All at once he knew the
reason. If Miranda had married little Cousin Denley
never in a hundred years would she have fallen in love
with him. Oxenham was a very different matter. The
man had good looks, intelligence and, when he chose,
a very charming manner. Miranda's susceptibilities
could not withstand such attributes; she would be
desperately in love with him in no time, if she was not
so already, and he did not like the idea of that! He did

not like it at all! He was jealous of Oxenham! Miranda must love only him!

This realization hit him like an icy blast, so that he rocked back on his heels. He loved Miranda! Of course he did! He always had, as far back as his memory could stretch. But not as a sister! No, he had sisters enough to know that what he felt for her was a very different emotion from that which he felt for Sophia and the rest, something much warmer and more tender. He wanted her to be always by his side, for her gentleness and her adoration to be his alone. In short, he wanted her to be his wife. Those words spoken so hastily not many minutes since had been the absolute truth, even if he had not known it at the time; but the knowledge had come too late. He had bungled things appallingly, discounted Miranda's sensibilities so boorishly that he had lost her to Oxenham. Worse than that, she was now very angry with him and positively disliked him. Silently Peter cursed himself for being every sort of a fool as deep misery engulfed him. What could he do? What could he say?

"Have you no answer to my question?" Miranda's voice brought him back to painful reality.

"Your question? Oh yes. Denley and—and—" He struggled to reassemble his thoughts. "I object because—because Oxenham has left too many broken hearts behind him. He does not love you sufficiently."

"I do not know what makes you an authority on that last subject, but I believe his lordship loves me in his own way."

"And what of your attachment to him?" The moment the words were out of Peter's mouth he regretted them, for her answer could only increase his pain.

"That is none of your business, but if you must know I like and respect him, and even if your opinion of him is very low I consider he has many admirable qualities."

Such a dispassionate reply should have cheered Peter, but instead, knowing her capacity for affection and the fact that she was totally lost to him, he found himself becoming angry.

"Like? Respect? Admirable qualities? What a fine parcel of goods you are getting for yourself! You know very well that with your tender heart you will get excessively attached to him, and then what will happen?"

"It will be a very good thing if I do come to love Oxenham, a very good thing indeed. It will make for much happiness in our marriage."

"Will it? And what will happen once he starts off with his bits of muslin again? What happiness will there be for you there? It will bring you only heartbreak and humiliation."

"Such a thing is not a foregone conclusion. If our love grows strong enough perhaps he will lose the taste for 'bits of muslin' as you so indelicately put it. Just because Oxenham has not had any enduring attachments so far does not mean that it is impossible. I think he has never had anyone to love and care for him. If I become his wife I intend to do both."

Imperceptibly their voices had been rising. Miranda's last statement goaded Peter into a jealous fury.

"No you will not!" he roared angrily. "For I will not have you loving him more than you do me! I will not have it, do you hear?" And he caught hold of Miranda, swinging her to face him for the first time.

Taken totally unawares she exclaimed, "Oh do not be so stupid!" then stopped with a gasp. Every note of her voice had expressed just how idiotic were his fears. Realizing that she had betrayed her true feelings so blatantly Miranda gave a cry and put her hands over her face to hide the tears that had started to fall once more.

"Miranda!" Peter's voice was no more than a whisper. He scarcely dared to believe what he had heard. "Miranda, does that mean that you do love me?"

"Oh go away, please," sobbed Miranda.

"No, no, give me an answer, I beg of you, and an honest one. Do you love me?" He drew her towards him until she was held tightly in his arms, so that the only refuge for her tear-stained face was to bury it against his shoulder.

"Of course I do, you great zany!" she sobbed.

"Oh thank goodness! I was afraid that you did not!" Peter was forced to close his eyes for a moment and to hold Miranda even more tightly. He was finding that relief can make a man just as sick and giddy as seasickness. Fortunately recovery is swifter. "Oh that was such a fright you gave me. Do not do such a thing to me again, I beg of you, or I fear I shall go totally distracted. Dearest girl, will you ever forgive me for making you weep so? I am a clumsy, blind fool, who does not deserve your love. I beg you to stop crying so that I can tell you how much I love you in return."

"Why did you not say you loved me before?" wept Miranda, her face still against his shoulder.

"Sheer stupidity," admitted Peter. "Though in my own defence I must say that since I cannot remember a time when I did not love you it was exceedingly difficult to recognize the state. Was that why you refused to marry me?"

"Of course."

"Not if I were the last man in the world. That was what you said. If you had hit me over the head with a cudgel you could not have dealt me a greater hurt."

"I thought that you were offering for me just because you disliked Oxenham so much and mistrusted him."

"So did I, my darling, at least as I spoke the words. I soon saw the truth, though, that I was jealous of him and so afraid that he would take you away from me. But be honest, you were quite prepared to wed simply to get Richard out of a tricky situation—or at least to wed anyone other than me. That was hard of you."

Gently he stroked the disorder of Miranda's hair, and his lips sought the nape of her neck.

"If it was, then I am sorry." Miranda's gentle voice was far from steady. "I thought that I would marry anyone for Richard's sake, even Mr. Denley if things got desperate enough, but when you offered in so casual a fashion, as if you did not care at all—and I cared so much—no, not even for Richard could I have done such a thing."

"I shall never forgive myself for my callous foolishness. I promise that I shall atone for it for the rest of my life by making you supremely happy, yet if I had not been such a blustering, unthinking fellow I might never have come to see how much I do love you. You did not help me, you know, for you were always throwing Miss Bella in my way. No wonder I could not recognize the state of my own heart."

"I have always known that I love you, with no prompting from anyone." Miranda turned her face towards him so that his kisses could find their target more easily. "But I never expected you to wed me, I thought such a thing to be quite impossible. I wanted you to be settled with a wife and family of your own, for you are never truly happy unless you are romping with a horde of children."

"And so you would have packed me off with Bella Wordsworth-Pugh, charming creature though she is, and never given me an opportunity to find out that I was really desperately in love with you. What a hard scheming female you are, but I have defeated your plotting and conniving, have I not? And as for being truly happy, I intend to be just that, if you are with me, and we will have such a time of it, filling New Place with children and moth-eaten dogs and half-mad magpies, and live in such wonderful chaos that even your Great-Aunt Evangeline will seem quite staid by comparison. Just think, I might have avoided it all if Oxenham had not come along and made me so insanely jealous. I suppose I must owe him a debt of gratitude. What will the poor fellow do now that you are going to marry me?''

''You have not proposed to me yet, so I have not accepted,'' pointed out Miranda, whose tears were rapidly abating.

''Well, if you marry me,'' amended Peter hastily.

''He has his yacht and the sea. I fancy that they are his only really constant loves, in spite of what I said earlier. Though I should hate to distress him I am convinced that his suffering will not last long, particularly once he commences his voyage to the Mediterranean.''

''Poor fellow, I almost pity him, though I was ready to wring his neck not ten minutes since. Have you quite finished crying? Then have my handkerchief, you have thoroughly soaked your own. Are you composed enough to discuss marriage now? I suppose Oxenham came all prepared with poetic speeches and the like.''

''No, he did not,'' replied Miranda, obediently wiping her eyes. ''In fact, none of my proposals have been the least bit romantic, which is most disappointing."

"None of your proposals? How many have you had?" cried Peter.

"Counting yours—if one can call it a proposal—I have had three of late, and so far yours is by far the worst. I do trust there will be a great improvement in your second attempt. I would dearly like to hear how much you love me, so I beg of you to continue."

Peter was startled at this revelation but a Kerswell was always equal to any challenge so he did indeed continue.

"Nothing will give me greater joy than telling you how much I love you. I shall repeat it ten times daily for the next fifty years at least, until you are heartily sick of hearing it. And as for proposals, you shall have the most romantic that can be devised. Would you like me to climb up to your window tonight and woo you by moonlight, or shall I go down on one knee to beg you to be my wife?"

But Miranda knew exactly what sort of a proposal she wanted. In the space of half an hour her spirits had gone from the deepest misery she had known to the heights of a happiness she had never expected to experience. Now Peter was closer to her, his cheek was against hers and his arms encircled her as if he would never let her go again. To Miranda this was total bliss, and she was afraid to disturb this moment of unbelievable joy, even for the most romantic manner of proposals.

"We are so comfortable as we are, my love, that I have no wish to move," she said softly, her arms stealing shyly about his neck. "I think that for you to propose just like this would do very well, for this is the most wonderful moment of my whole life and I can think of nothing more romantic than to hear you say you love me."

"I agree," replied Peter tensely. "Oh my darling Miranda, how I agree!"

IN THE PASSAGE Nanny Hart still stood sentinel outside Miranda's door. The promised ten minutes were up long since, but Nanny's small stature had brought her ear conveniently close to the keyhole for her to overhear much of the conversation within, and if anyone was going to interrupt Miss Miranda's happiness it certainly would not be Nanny Hart.

Banks came creeping up the stairs on tiptoe.

"How are things, Mrs. Hart?" he asked anxiously. "Is Miss Miranda feeling better? Is there anything I can do?"

"It is kind of you to ask, Mr. Banks," answered Nanny, whisking a joyful tear from her eye, "but everything is absolutely splendid—though if you really want to do something may I suggest you see to it that the cushions on the library sofa are plumped up and comfortable, because, by my guess, given a half-hour or so Sir Henry is going to feel the need for another lie down."

Take 4 bestselling love stories FREE

Plus get a FREE surprise gift!

Special Limited-time Offer

Harlequin Reader Service®

Mail to

In the U.S.
3010 Walden Avenue
P.O. Box 1867
Buffalo, N.Y. 14269-1867

In Canada
P.O. Box 609
Fort Erie, Ontario
L2A 5X3

YES! Please send me 4 free Harlequin Regency Romance™ novels and my free surprise gift. Then send me 4 brand-new novels every other month. Bill me at the low price of $2.49* each—a savings of 26¢ apiece off cover prices. There are no shipping, handling or other hidden costs. I understand that accepting the books and gift places me under no obligation ever to buy any books. I can always return a shipment and cancel at any time. Even if I never buy another book from Harlequin, the 4 free books and the surprise gift are mine to keep forever.

*Offer slightly different in Canada—$2.49 per book plus 49¢ per shipment for delivery. Sales tax applicable in N.Y. Canadian residents add applicable federal and provincial sales tax.

248 BPA 4AJX (US)   348 BPA 4A73 (CAN)

Name   (PLEASE PRINT)

Address   Apt. No.

City   State/Prov.   Zip/Postal Code

This offer is limited to one order per household and not valid to present Harlequin Regency Romance™ subscribers. Terms and prices are subject to change.

REG-BPADR   © 1990 Harlequin Enterprises Limited

Coming soon
to an easy chair near you.

FIRST CLASS is Harlequin's armchair travel plan for the incurably romantic. You'll visit a different dreamy destination every month from January through December without ever packing a bag. No jet lag, no expensive air fares and *no* lost luggage. Just First Class Harlequin Romance reading, featuring exotic settings from Tasmania to Thailand, from Egypt to Australia, and more.

FIRST CLASS romantic excursions guaranteed! Start your world tour in January. Look for the special **FIRST CLASS** destination on selected Harlequin Romance titles—there's a new one every month.

NEXT DESTINATION:
THAILAND

 Harlequin Books

JTR2

HARLEQUIN'S "BIG WIN"
SWEEPSTAKES RULES & REGULATIONS
NO PURCHASE NECESSARY TO ENTER OR RECEIVE A PRIZE

1. To enter and join the Reader Service, scratch off the metallic strips on all your BIG WIN tickets #1-#6. This will reveal the values for each sweepstakes entry number, the number of free book(s) you will receive and your free bonus gift as part of our Reader Service. If you do not wish to take advantage of our Reader Service but wish to enter the Sweepstakes only, scratch off the metallic strips on your BIG WIN tickets #1-#4. Return your entire sheet of tickets intact. Incomplete and/or inaccurate entries are ineligible for that section or sections of prizes. Not responsible for mutilated or unreadable entries or inadvertent printing errors. Mechanically reproduced entries are null and void.

2. Whether you take advantage of this offer or not, your Sweepstakes numbers will be compared against the list of winning numbers generated at random by the computer. In the event that all prizes are not claimed by March 31, 1992, a random drawing will be held from all qualified entries received from March 30, 1990 to March 31, 1992, to award all unclaimed prizes. All cash prizes (Grand to Sixth), will be mailed to the winners and are payable by check in U.S. funds. Seventh prize will be shipped to winners via third-class mail. These prizes are in addition to any free, surprise or mystery gifts that might be offered. Versions of this sweepstakes with different prizes of approximate equal value may appear at retail outlets or in other mailings by Torstar Corp. and its affiliates.

3. The following prizes are awarded in this sweepstakes: ★ Grand Prize (1) $1,000,000; First Prize (1) $25,000; Second Prize (1) $10,000; Third Prize (5) $5,000; Fourth Prize (10) $1,000; Fifth Prize (100) $250; Sixth Prize (2,500) $10; ★ ★ Seventh Prize (6,000) $12.95 ARV.

   ★ This presentation offers a Grand Prize of a $1,000,000 annuity. Winner will receive $33,333.33 a year for 30 years without interest totalling $1,000,000.

   ★ ★ Seventh Prize: A fully illustrated hardcover book published by Torstar Corp. Approximate retail value of the book is $12.95.

   Entrants may cancel the Reader Service at anytime without cost or obligation to buy (see details in center insert card).

4. This Sweepstakes is being conducted under the supervision of an independent judging organization. By entering this Sweepstakes, each entrant accepts and agrees to be bound by these rules and the decisions of the judges, which shall be final and binding. Odds of winning in the random drawing are dependent upon the total number of entries received. Taxes, if any, are the sole responsibility of the winners. Prizes are nontransferable. All entries must be received at the address printed on the reply card and must be postmarked no later than 12:00 MIDNIGHT on March 31, 1992. The drawing for all unclaimed sweepstakes prizes will take place May 30, 1992, at 12:00 NOON, at the offices of Marden-Kane, Inc., Lake Success, New York.

5. This offer is open to residents of the U.S., the United Kingdom, France and Canada, 18 years or older, except employees and their immediate family members of Torstar Corp., its affiliates, subsidiaries, and all other agencies and persons connected with the use, marketing or conduct of this sweepstakes. All Federal, State, Provincial and local laws apply. Void wherever prohibited or restricted by law. Any litigation within the Province of Quebec respecting the conduct and awarding of a prize in this publicity contest must be submitted to the Régie des loteries et courses du Québec.

6. Winners will be notified by mail and may be required to execute an affidavit of eligibility and release, which must be returned within 14 days after notification or an alternative winner will be selected. Canadian winners will be required to correctly answer an arithmetical skill-testing question administered by mail, which must be returned within a limited time. Winners consent to the use of their names, photographs and/or likenesses for advertising and publicity in conjunction with this and similar promotions without additional compensation. For a list of major winners, send a stamped, self-addressed envelope to: WINNERS LIST, c/o Harlequin Reader Service, 3010 Walden Ave., P.O. Box 1396, Buffalo, NY 14269-1396. Winners Lists will be fulfilled after the May 30, 1992 drawing date.

If Sweepstakes entry form is missing, please print your name and address on a 3″ ×5″ piece of plain paper and send to:

In the U.S.
Harlequin's "BIG WIN" Sweepstakes
3010 Walden Ave.
P.O. Box 1867
Buffalo, NY 14269-1867

In Canada
Harlequin's "BIG WIN" Sweepstakes
P.O. Box 609
Fort Erie, Ontario
L2A 5X3

Offer limited to one per household.
© 1991 Harlequin Enterprises Limited   Printed in the U.S.A.

LTY-H191R

HARLEQUIN
American Romance®

RELIVE THE MEMORIES...

From New York's immigrant experience to the Great Quake of 1906. From the Western Front of World War I to the Roaring Twenties. From the indomitable spirit of the thirties to the home front of the Fabulous Forties. From the baby boom fifties to the Woodstock Nation sixties... A CENTURY OF AMERICAN ROMANCE takes you on a nostalgic journey through the twentieth century.

Revel in the romance of a time gone by... and sneak a peek at romance in a exciting future.

Watch for all the A CENTURY OF AMERICAN ROMANCE titles coming to you one per month over the next three months in Harlequin American Romance.

Don't miss February's A CENTURY OF AMERICAN ROMANCE title, #377—TILL THE END OF TIME by Elise Title.

A CENTURY OF
AMERICAN ROMANCE
1970s

The women...the men...the passions...the memories...

Harlequin Intrigue®

A SPAULDING & DARIEN MYSTERY
by Robin Francis

An engaging pair of amateur sleuths—Jenny Spaulding and Peter Darien—were introduced to Harlequin Intrigue readers in #147, BUTTON, BUTTON (Oct. 1990). Jenny and Peter will return for further spine-chilling romantic adventures in April 1991 in #159, DOUBLE DARE in which they solve their next puzzling mystery. Two other books featuring Jenny and Peter will follow in the A SPAULDING AND DARIEN MYSTERY series.

IBB-1A